Bernard William Kelly

Life of Henry Benedict Stuart, Cardinal Duke of York

With a Notice of Rome in his Time

Bernard William Kelly

Life of Henry Benedict Stuart, Cardinal Duke of York
With a Notice of Rome in his Time

ISBN/EAN: 9783744764100

Printed in Europe, USA, Canada, Australia, Japan

Cover: Foto ©Raphael Reischuk / pixelio.de

More available books at **www.hansebooks.com**

Pompeo Batoni pinxit.

HENRY BENEDICT STUART, CARDINAL DUKE OF YORK.

LIFE

OF

HENRY BENEDICT STUART,

CARDINAL DUKE OF YORK.

With a Notice of Rome in his Time.

BY

BERNARD W. KELLY.

R. & T. WASHBOURNE,
18 PATERNOSTER ROW, LONDON.
BENZIGER BROS.: NEW YORK, CINCINNATI, AND CHICAGO.
1899.

Nihil Obstat:

J. OSWALD TURNER, O.J.,
CENSOR DEPUTATUS.

Imprimatur:

HERBERTUS CARDINALIS VAUGHAN,
ARCHIEPISCOPUS WESTMONASTERIENSIS.

To

FATHER CUTHBERT, O.S.B.,

IN SÆCULO,

HERBERT CONSTABLE,

THIS LITTLE WORK WAS DEDICATED ;

BUT ERE ITS PAGES WERE COMPLETED

HIS SOUL HAD PASSED AWAY TO THAT 'FAR, FAR GREATER REST,'

ON THE FEAST OF THE DEDICATION

OF THE BASILICA OF SS. PETER AND PAUL,

NOVEMBER THE EIGHTEENTH, 1898.

PREFACE.

IN the following little work will be found the leading events connected with the life of Henry Benedict, the Cardinal Duke of York, and last direct descendant of the unfortunate House of Stuart.

While narrating matters of purely personal interest, the writer has deemed it advisable to add a brief outline of such contemporary events as bear more or less directly on the subject of this memoir.

The writer tenders his best thanks to those who have encouraged and assisted him in drawing up this account, especially to the Rev. R. McCoy, S.J., of Stonyhurst College, Lancashire, who has supplied valuable information concerning Prince Henry's Cardinalate, and to the Rev. Oswald Turner, C.J., of St. George's College, Weybridge, who has kindly revised the manuscript. His acknowledgments are likewise due to his old friend Mr. George Williams, of Erdington, for kindly criticisms and suggestions.

In conclusion it may be remarked that the frontispiece is from a photograph by Messrs. Walker and Boutall, permission to reproduce which has been kindly granted by Lionel Cust, Esq., Director of the National Portrait Gallery.

January, 1899.

CONTENTS.

LIFE

OF

HENRY BENEDICT STUART,

CARDINAL DUKE OF YORK

PART I.

1725-1747.

OLUMES have been written on the life of Prince Charles Edward, the Young Pretender. His daring and chivalrous attempt in 1745 to recover the crown of his ancestors, with all the circumstances of that memorable campaign — the victory at Preston Pans, the brilliant march to Derby, and the final rout at Culloden, where Stuart hopes and Highland clanship fell for ever—are cameos of history on which generations of readers and students have gazed with wonder, admiration and delight. Of his brother, Prince Henry Benedict Stuart, few know any more than that he was a Cardinal and Bishop of Frascati, that he led a simple and unostentatious life, and finally died, unknown to fame, at an advanced age. In the following pages it has been our endeavour to add to this meagre stock of information by the publication of further details regarding this by no means unimportant or uninteresting personage.

Henry Benedict Stuart, Cardinal Duke of York, the last representative in the direct male line of the Royal House of Stuart, was born at Rome, in the Palazzo Muti Savorelli, situated in the Via Santi Apostoli, and still known by the name of the Palazzo del Pretendente, on March 6, 1725, four years after the birth of his elder brother, Charles Edward, the Young Pretender, and thirty-seven years after his grandfather, James II., had been driven from the British throne. The palace in which the Cardinal Duke was born, which is represented in a contemporary picture by Van Lint as a large square mansion of stone standing in its own extensive pleasure-grounds, was given to the Stuarts by Pope Clement XI. in 1717. The father of Prince Henry was James Francis Edward Stuart, generally known as the Old Pretender, but known to the Jacobites as James III. James Francis Edward Stuart, the son of James II., by Mary, daughter of the Duke of Modena, was born in St. James's Palace, London, on June 10, 1688, a few months before the outbreak of the Revolution that banished the Stuart family from these realms for ever. On the death of his father at St. Germains in 1701, James Francis Edward was at once recognised as King by a large body of adherents in the British Isles, and also by Louis XIV. of France, who in 1708 fitted out an unsuccessful expedition to Scotland in his behalf. Seven years later, when Prince George, Elector of Hanover, ascended the throne of England, the exiled James Francis Edward landed in Scotland, and at his presence the abortive rebellion of 1715 broke out. The Chevalier de St. George, as James is sometimes called, was not qualified to act as leader in such an enterprise, and he soon found it expedient to re-embark for France, leaving his party in a state of thorough disorganization, and the scaffold wet with the blood of Derwentwater and Kenmure and a number of less distinguished followers. In 1717 he settled in Rome, a city ever afterwards associated with the events that marked the closing scenes in the great Stuart drama. His wife, Maria Clementina, was the daughter of Prince James Sobieski, son of the renowned John Sobieski, King of Poland, who, by the wisdom of his counsels and the prowess of his arms, delivered Austria, and perhaps all central Europe, from the threatened domination of the Turks. The romantic and impressionable character of the Princess frequently led her, when a child, to predict her future elevation to the throne of England, a prophecy which seemed to be in a fair way towards realization when, at the age of seventeen, she was betrothed to the titular James III. As the English Government was known to be much opposed to this union, the greatest care was necessary to prevent the intended marriage from being frustrated by political intrigues. To Mr. Charles Wogan, an Irish officer in the French service, and a man of great courage and diplomatic skill, was entrusted the task of conducting the lovely Princess to Bologna, where the Chevalier had for the time fixed his court. Wogan, with his assistants, Majors Gaydon and O'Toole, carried the perilous undertaking to a successful issue. A medal, bearing the motto ' Deceptis Custodibus,' and as device a chariot in full speed, was struck to commemorate the royal elope-

ment, the fame of which was soon spread over Europe.
But, although the Princess arrived in Bologna in the
month of May, the marriage, owing to the Chevalier's
absence in Madrid, did not take place till September.

On the evening of December 31, 1720, the stillness
of the Eternal City was broken by the artillery of the
Castle of St. Angelo, announcing the birth of the
titular Prince of Wales. The event was celebrated
with bonfires and illuminations, and the Cardinal
Protectors of the various European Powers paid State
visits to the child, who, five hours after his birth, was
baptized under the name of Charles Edward Louis
Casimir by his Lordship the Bishop of Montifiascone,
in the Church of the Santi Apostoli. A great concourse of noble and distinguished personages, including
seven Cardinals and fourteen British Peers, were
present at this ceremony, which was depicted in a
large painting now in the possession of the Earl of
Northesk.

The subject of this sketch, the second son of the
Old Chevalier, was born on March 6, 1725. The
happy event was immediately communicated to the
reigning Pontiff, Benedict XIII., who, at the time of
the announcement, was engaged in private devotion
in his oratory. The Holy Father, having graciously
intimated that he would himself baptize the child, at
once proceeded to the palace of the Stuarts, where he
was received by the Chevalier in person, and ushered
into the apartment where the Princess lay. James
took the infant into his arms, and presented it to the
Pope, saying as he did so: ' I present to your Holiness
the Duke of York, that you may make him a Christian.'

The Pontiff thereupon performed the rite of holy baptism, giving the little Duke the names of Henry Benedict Clement Mary Edward, with other names up to the number of twelve. The visit of the Sovereign Pontiff was quickly followed by that of the whole College of Cardinals, who came in all their stately splendour to congratulate the ' King and Queen of England ' on the birth of their second son.

At the time of Prince Henry's birth his father and mother were unhappily estranged from each other by a combination of circumstances brought about in great measure by the suspicious character and wayward conduct of Clementina. During the years that intervened between the birth of his first son, Charles Edward, and that of the Duke of York, James had been planning another rising in Scotland, and had been in frequent correspondence with some of the leading Jacobites on the Continent, of whom Atterbury, the exiled Bishop of Rochester, and Lord Oxford were the most noted. To facilitate his negotiations, the Chevalier had taken into his personal service a certain Colonel John Hay, on whom he conferred the title of Earl of Inverness. Lady Hay was appointed to the household of the Queen, and her brother, James Murray, was created governor to the Prince of Wales. In the discharge of his duties as royal courier, Lord Inverness had reason to suspect that the Earl of Mar, James's general in the Rebellion, was betraying the secrets of the Stuart Court to the British Government, and he laid his fears before the titular King, who mentioned them to his Queen. Clementina, who had absolute faith in the abilities and fidelity of Mar, flew into a violent passion, charged

Lord Inverness with seeking to bring about Mar's ruin, and insisted that Inverness and all the members of his family should be dismissed from the Stuart Court. In vain did the Chevalier protest against the unfounded charges of the Queen, and her still more unreasonable demands. Clementina was deaf to all argument; on James's steadily refusing to banish his faithful Hay, she declared her intention of retiring to a convent, a threat which she put into execution on November 15, 1725, when, accompanied by Lady Southesk, she withdrew to the Ursuline Convent of St. Cecilia in Trastevere.

It does not come within the scope of this little work to follow this miserable dispute through its many details, or to narrate how the representations of Clementina made her for the time appear in the eyes of the world as the victim of conjugal tyranny. Harmony was restored in 1727, when Lord Inverness, by a rare display of generosity and zeal for the interests of his Sovereign, prevailed on James to dispense with his services, in order that the quarrel, which had now reached the proportions of a scandal, might be speedily brought to an end. Owing to the absence in France of the Chevalier, who was preparing for another insurrection in the Highlands, the reconciliation, if such it may be termed, did not take place till February, 1728, when Clementina left the convent and rejoined her consort at Bologna.

It is pleasant to turn from this unfortunate quarrel to the subject which occupied so much of the Chevalier's solicitude—the education of his sons. As long as her health permitted, Clementina herself undertook this important duty, a task for which she was fitted by the extent of her information and the vigour of her mind. It had been the original intention of James III. to place his sons under the tuition of Sir Andrew Ramsay, better known as the Chevalier Ramsay, the great Scotch scholar and educationalist, who had been converted to the Catholic Church by the immortal François de Salignac Fénelon, Archbishop of Cambray. But the dissensions reigning in the Stuart household, in consequence of the unhappy incident narrated above, had made the residence of Ramsay at the Palazzo dei Santi Apostoli impossible. His place was supplied, so far as the loss of such an instructor, whose fame as a scholar was familiar all over Europe, could be supplied, by Sir Thomas Sheridan and the Abbé Legouz, of the University of Paris. Under these preceptors the two princes went through a complete course of what was then termed the belles-lettres, though their English education seems, in the case of Prince Charles at least, to have been somewhat neglected. They both spoke, however, the French and Italian languages with grace and fluency. When the Abbé Legouz resigned his charge, they continued their studies under Drs. Berkeley and Cooper, two nonjuring Anglican clergymen who acted as chaplains to the Protestant members of the Chevalier's Court.

Of the childhood of the future Cardinal few particulars are forthcoming. At one time it was the intention of James to have him brought up at Madrid, in order that the sympathy and influence of the Escuriel might be enlisted on behalf of his family in any future attempt to regain the British throne. This scheme was never carried out, owing to the strong opposition of Clementina, whose maternal affection and dread of dangerous surroundings made her determined never to consent to separation from her children.

James Field-Marshal Keith, the 'noble exile' whose death at Hochkirchen, in the Seven Years' War, has been described by Lord Macaulay in a well-known passage, gives us, in a letter to his brother, George Lord Marischal, dated November 21, 1731, a glimpse of Prince Henry when in his seventh year. It runs thus:

'The little Duke is much on his good behaviour. He has ordered a journal of his actions to be kept and given me, that you may see how well he behaves. I never saw any child comparable to him. His brother has already got the better of his governors, which makes him a little unruly; but I fancy he will be bold and no dissembler—two great and good qualities.'

In another letter, of October 30, 1732, the Marshal says:

'The Duke of York believes I send you a journal of his actions; he stands in great awe of it, lest his faults should be published in Europe and Asia, and is very fond to do any good thing to be put in the journal.' This letter was written from Rome.

Lord Inverness (Colonel Hay), in a letter to Thomas Gordon, Admiral of the Russian Fleet and Governor of Cronstadt, bears witness to the good impression made by Charles and Henry on their friends, and further says that 'They are the most lively boys this day on earth; pray God preserve them long,' etc. The natural cheerfulness of Prince Henry, which never forsook him through life, led the poet Gray, some eight years later, when the future Cardinal was in his sixteenth year, to describe him as having 'more spirit' than his elder brother.

In 1733 events in Poland inspired some of the Continental Jacobites with the hope that the influence of the Court of France and the family alliance of the Stuarts with the Sobieskis might have the effect of securing the crown of that unhappy country for the young Duke of York. In February of that year died Augustus, Elector of Saxony, who had been summoned to the throne of the Jagellons by the voice of the Polish Diet in 1697, on the death of the great John Sobieski.

In March the Chevalier wrote to Prince James Sobieski, expressing his pleasure at the favourable disposition of certain influential persons in Warsaw towards his family, but also reminding him of the practical impossibility of securing the election of a child of eight to the throne of a country proverbial for the turbulence of its factions. In the event the crown went to Augustus, son of the previous monarch, who, soldier though he was, could not take possession of his kingdom till his adversaries had been awed into submission by the presence of 60,000 Russian bayonets.

The year 1735 opened with a great blow for the Chevalier and his family, in the loss of Queen Clementina, who expired, after a long and painful illness, on Tuesday, January 18. After the reconciliation already recorded, James III. and his consort had continued to reside together at Rome, though the deep mutual love which had characterized their early wedded life had never been quite restored. The Chevalier, absorbed in schemes for another invasion of Britain, was too preoccupied to attend much to matters of domestic interest, while Clementina, on her part, made no earnest attempts to regain that place in her husband's affections which she had in a great measure lost by her own foolish and unreasonable conduct. She spent her last years chiefly in works of piety and charity, assisting poor girls who were in danger from evil surroundings, relieving destitute families, and establishing needlework guilds among the Roman ladies for supplying needy churches with vestments and altar linen. She was encouraged in these admirable undertakings by her confessor, the celebrated Franciscan preacher who did so much to revive religious fervour in Italy, Father Leonard, of Port Maurice, who was beatified by Pope Pius VI. in 1796, and canonized by Pope Pius IX. in 1867. Pope Clement XII., to show his esteem for the deceased, and the goodwill he entertained towards the Stuart family, ordered a most sumptuous funeral for the Princess, some account of which may not be considered out of place here.

The body of the Princess was taken on the day of her death to the Church of the Santi Apostoli, the hearse being accompanied by the ladies and gentlemen of the household and a number of servants and attendants, bearing funeral torches and wax candles. As the deceased, shortly before her death, had become a Tertiary of the Order of St. Dominic, a number of the Dominican Fathers met the corpse at the entrance of the church, and conducted it in procession to a bed of state, surrounded by twenty-four wax candles, where

it lay while the Office for the Dead was chanted by the
choir.   This was followed by the ceremony of embalmment, which took place in an inner apartment,
probably the sacristy, under the direction of Signor
Antonio Leprotti, private physician to the Pope, in
the presence of the Duchess Strozzi, her Excellency
Donna Isabella Aquaviva d'Aragona, and, by special
dispensation, the pontifical majordomo, Monsignor
Gamberucci, Archbishop of Amasia.   At the conclusion of this Office, the ladies attired the body
in the habit of the Dominican nuns, after which
it was conducted to the chapel of the Father Minister-
General, where a captain and company of the Swiss
Guard kept watch round the catafalque.

On Sunday, the 23rd, about noon, the ladies-in-
waiting removed the religious habit from the deceased,
putting on in its place royal robes of purple velvet,
gold, and ermine.   It was then conducted, with much
solemnity, to the Church of the Apostles, which was
suitably adorned with funeral emblems and insignia.
Thirty-two Cardinals, in their violet mourning robes,
attended, and assisted at the Office for the Dead,
which was chanted by the Mendicant Friars.   The
remains were then taken in procession to St. Peter's,
attended by members of numerous Religious Orders
and Congregations, bearing lighted candles, and
followed by the entire Stuart household in Court
dress.   With the hearse also went the students of
the English, Scotch, and Irish colleges, and a detachment of the Swiss Guard.   Then followed in order
the officials of the Pope's household, Prelates of the
Palace, Masters of Ceremonies, Protonotaries, and
Chaplains in their carriages, attended by halberdiers

and mace-bearers with silver maces. Last of all came
ten coaches, containing the Chevalier de St. George,
the Princes Charles Edward and Henry, and their
respective suites. At seven in the evening the procession entered St. Peter's, where the body was
conducted to the choir, which, by order of his
Eminence Cardinal St. Clement, Archpriest of the
Fabric, had been adorned with hangings of black
velvet and gold tassels and shields, bearing the arms
and monogram of the deceased Princess. The choir
was illuminated by great wax candles, set in massive
silver candlesticks. After the *De Profundis* had
been recited by Monsignor Cervini, Patriarch of
Jerusalem and Canon of St. Peter's, the body was
again stripped of its royal robes, clothed in the
Dominican habit, and enclosed with the regalia in
an inner and an outer coffin. Next morning a
solemn Mass of Requiem was sung by the Cardinal
Archpriest, in the presence of the Chevalier and his
family, several Cardinals, the Archbishop of Hiero-
polis, the Bishops of Cyrene, Constance and Marciana.
After the Absolution had been given, the clergy and
court, preceded by the cross, attended the coffin to
the vaults, where it was placed in the crypt near the
Chapel of the Presentation. The heart of the deceased
was enclosed in a silver urn, and deposited in the
Church of the Apostles, where a handsome monument,
erected by the Bishop of the Fabric of St. Peter's,
marks the spot where it is laid.

We now pass from the purely domestic concerns of
the exiled family to a consideration of the events
connected with the last Jacobite rebellion in Scotland.
Though these occurrences are not immediately con-

nected with the subject of the present memoir, some
reference must be made to them to enable the reader
to understand and appreciate the circumstances of
the times in which Prince Henry lived.

In 1741 the unjust aggression of the sovereign of
a then unimportant German State involved half of
Europe in a bloody struggle. The death of the
Emperor Charles VI., in the October of the preceding
year, had presented to Frederick of Prussia a favourable opportunity for marching a powerful army into
the Austrian dominions, and annexing the province
of Silesia to his territories. The 'Moriamur pro rege
nostra Maria Theresa' of the indignant Hungarian
nobles as they raised their flashing sabres in defence
of the insulted daughter of the Cæsars and the rights
of her infant son, their sovereign, sounded the note
of war which was to devastate the greater part of
Europe for seven years. Alone of all the Powers that
had sworn to safeguard the claims of the Empress,
England remained faithful to its word, and in 1743
the broken faith of France and Bavaria, who, regard-
less of treaties, had supported the aggression of
Frederick, received condign punishment in a crushing
defeat from the British forces at Dettingen. It was
at this juncture that Cardinal Tencin, Prime Minister
of France, resolved to divert the attention of England
by a Stuart rising at home. He invited Prince Charles
to Paris, assuring him that an army of 15,000 men
and a fleet of transports would be put at his disposal.
The young Prince, to whom the prospect of regaining
the throne of his fathers had become the one object
of life, was not slow to avail himself of the promise
thus made. He hastened to Paris to place himself at

the head of the armament, but, alas! the elements, ever the foes of the House of Stuart, once more declared against them. A violent tempest covered the northern coasts of France with the wreckage of the invading flotilla, and the young Chevalier was constrained to await a more favourable opportunity.

It is from the pen of Father Julius Cordara, of the Society of Jesus, an intimate friend of Cardinal York, that we know of the full details of Charles Edward's secret departure from Rome. While living at Albano with his father, many years afterwards, Cardinal York made Cordara's acquaintance. The Jesuit met the Duke of York as his Eminence was taking a walk one evening on the beautiful road between Castel Gandolfo and Albano. The Cardinal entered into conversation with him, took a fancy to him, and became his close friend. After his consecration as Bishop of Frascati, the Cardinal Duke often had Cordara with him on prolonged visits, and though the Cardinal consulted him on many matters of importance, the Jesuit never forgot his patron's double rank as ecclesiastical and temporal Prince, and treated him always with becoming reverence.

At the time the young Chevalier left Rome, the war of the Austrian succession was at its height. The Mediterranean literally swarmed with English men-of-war, and a multitude of spies were to be found everywhere, ready to chronicle the Chevalier's movements, so that it was necessary for him to exercise the utmost caution in making his way to the French capital. On January 9, 1744, he left Rome for Cisterna, about thirty miles distant on the Via Appia, where he had a shooting-box. The day before his departure from Rome, the Prince gave an entertainment to the leading nobility, and during the whole course of the evening did not betray, by the slightest look or word, the fact that he was on the eve of commencing a war against one of the most powerful monarchs of Europe.

He ordered a carriage to be ready to start shortly after midnight, explaining that he wished to have some sport early on the following day. The whole scheme was kept so profound a secret that not even the Duke of York, who usually shared his brother's counsels, was aware of the true nature of the project.

At the appointed hour the young Chevalier drove out of Rome, accompanied by Sir Thomas Sheridan, and when some distance out in the country was met by a Mr. Stafford, one of his gentlemen-in-waiting, with two horses saddled and bridled. Charles now expressed his intention of riding to Cisterna by the Albano road. He and Sheridan therefore mounted the horses, and, bidding the coachman drive back to the city, galloped off for some distance, and, after allowing time for the carriage to get well on its way, retraced their path, and made for the Tuscan road by another route. At Capraola, where Cardinal Acquaviva had a palace, they found relays of horses, and after five days' travelling reached Genoa, whence the Prince and his companion sailed to the adjacent shore of France in a rowing-boat, to avoid arousing the suspicions of the numerous British cruisers sailing about the coast.

In the meantime the Duke of York had received intelligence of the scheme, but, for the sake of preserving his brother's secret more effectually, pretended

to be greatly alarmed on not finding Charles at
Cisterna. While he was giving orders for inquiries to
be made as to the delay, Mr. Stafford, who was in the
plot, came in with the news that Prince Charles had
met with an accident, caused by the slipping of his
horse, and had been taken to the palace of the King,
their father, at Albano. Lest news of the mishap
should reach his father's ears, the Duke gave strict
orders that nothing should be said about the matter;
but, notwithstanding the prohibition, the story spread,
and was believed by everyone. After a few days,
Prince Henry made preparations as though to visit
his brother, when a letter arrived from Stafford,
stating that His Royal Highness wished the hunt to
be transferred to Lake Fogliano, ten miles off, and
that the Prince would be there to take part in it.
When the Duke and his party arrived at Fogliano,
they found another letter from Stafford, in which it
was stated that the wound in the Prince's foot had
not quite healed, and that the doctor had ordered him
a few days' rest. Thus, several days more elapsed
before the truth became known, and by that time
Charles Edward was safe in France.

As the story of the rebellion of '45 belongs exclusively to the history of the young Chevalier, any
detailed account of that romantic episode would be
entirely out of place in a narrative dealing with the
Cardinal Duke of York. Still, we cannot let the last
heroic effort of the Stuart dynasty to recover its long-
lost throne pass entirely unnoticed.

Though the fleet destined for his service had been
destroyed, hope still remained, and on July 21, 1745,
Charles Edward and the Seven Men of Moidart stood

alone on the shores of Loch-na-Nuagh. Following the generous example of Cameron of Lochiel, the Highland clans rallied to the standard thus boldly unfurled, and once more unsheathed the sword on behalf of Scotland's ancient line. Then quickly followed the capture of Edinburgh, the festivities of Holyrood, where the young Chevalier won all hearts, and the glorious victory of Preston Pans, where the irresistible fury of the Highlanders swept Sir John Cope's army in rout and confusion from the field. Then came the march into England, the capture of Carlisle and Manchester, and the entrance into Derby on December 2. Nor was the retreat which the unsympathetic attitude of the great English houses, and the large forces that were advancing against him, made necessary less glorious to the Prince. At Clifton Moor, in Cumberland, the retreating Highlanders turned fiercely on their pursuers, and in the moonlight of a clear winter's night forced the Duke of Cumberland's dragoons to fall back with considerable loss. In Scotland one last triumph awaited them, to shed a departing ray of glory over the Stuart cause. On the evening of January 23, 1746, amidst a storm of wind and rain, a large army under General Hawley was signally defeated at Falkirk.

The Duke of Cumberland, George II.'s son, now arrived on the scene, at the head of powerful forces, and at the advance of their terrible assailant, the 'plaid-men' slowly continued their retreat northward. The councils of the Chevalier were distracted by dissensions, and his little army, worn out by famine and innumerable hardships, daily diminished in numbers. In this forlorn condition it was attacked by the whole English army at Culloden Moor, near Inverness, on April 16. Resorting to the simple tactics that had made them victorious on so many fields, the whole body of the clans (with the exception of one of the tribes of Macdonalds on the left), drawing their broadswords and covering themselves with their targets, precipitated themselves on the foe. A heavy and incessant fire of grapeshot and musketry rolled from the English lines on the advancing columns of the Highlanders, and the few shattered bands that burst through the first division of the Duke's army were immediately surrounded and cut to pieces.

The Young Adventurer fled from the field of his ruined hopes to the bleak valleys and snow-clad hills, where, for the space of five months, the descendant of Robert Bruce wandered, a proscribed fugitive, with a price of £30,000 on his head. That none of the poor peasantry among whom he lived offered to betray him, is as splendid an example of chivalrous honour and heroic loyalty as any recorded in history.

As soon as the suppression of the rebellion became known in Rome, the greatest anxiety prevailed in James's Court as to the safety of Prince Charles. As may easily be expected, the most contradictory and conflicting rumours reached, from time to time, the young Prince's father and friends. Now he was reported dead; at another time his safe arrival in France was announced; at another time he was said to be captured. By the express wish of James, public prayers were daily recited in the Church of the Santi Apostoli and elsewhere in Rome for the safe deliverance of his son from the perils that surrounded him.

The friends and followers of Prince Charles on the Continent were meanwhile exerting themselves to provide him with effective means for escape.

Shortly after the news of his brother's victory at Preston Pans, the Duke of York had arrived in Paris from Rome, with the intention of proceeding to England with a Franco-Jacobite army that was being organized. His presence in the French capital was now of service in encouraging the members of the Jacobite party resident there to make strenuous efforts to rescue Prince Charles from his dangerous position. By the exertions of the future Cardinal and his friends, a privateer was fitted out and despatched, and, after narrowly escaping capture from the English fleet, this vessel arrived safely in the waters of Loch-na-Nuagh, near the very spot where Charles, a year before, had sprung ashore, full of hope and courage, 'to carve a passage to the British throne.' The arrival of the friendly craft was communicated to the young Chevalier, who, several days later, came on board, 'his visage wan, and his constitution greatly impaired by famine and fatigue.' He generously delayed starting for two days longer, to give an opportunity to a number of his followers to come on board. About 150 persons availed themselves of this chance of escape, and on September 20 the vessel set sail. A thick fog, fortunately, enabled her to elude the vigilance of a squadron under Admiral Lestock, and the same good fortune preserved the exiles from capture by two other British men-of-war, and on the ninth day after weighing anchor the privateer and its precious freight reached the shores of France.

Journeying from the little seaport of Roscoff, where he had landed, Charles arrived at Morlaix, where he spent a few days in resting after the fatigues of the voyage. From this place he addressed a letter to his brother Henry, acquainting him of his safe return, and requesting him to inform the French King officially of the same. King Louis, on hearing the good news, ordered the Château of St. Antoine to be fitted up for the Prince's reception, while the Duke of York, accompanied by a retinue of French and Scottish noblemen and gentlemen, hastened to meet the brother who had so often been given up as lost. Shortly after their meeting, Prince Henry wrote the following account of it to his father. It is dated from his residence at Clichy, and runs thus :

' October 17, 1746.

' This very morning, after I writ you my last, I had the happiness of meeting with my dearest brother. He did not know me at first sight ; but I am sure I knew him very well, for he is not in the least altered since I saw him, except grown somewhat broader and fatter, which is incomprehensible after all the fatigues he has endured. Your Majesty may conceive better than I can express in writing the tenderness of our first meeting. Those that were present said they never saw the like in their lives, and, indeed, I defy the whole world to show another brother so kind and loving as he is to me. . . . The Prince sees and will scarcely see anybody but myself for a few days, that he may have a little time for rest before he is plagued by all the world, as to be sure he will when once he sees company. I go every day to dine with him. Yesterday I brought him privately to see my house, and I perceive he has as much *goût* for the chase as ever he had. Most humbly asking your Majesty's blessing,

> ' I remain,
>> ' Your most dutiful son,
>>> '.HENRY.'

Charles remained at the Castle of St. Antoine, near Clichy, for a few days, to recruit himself and make preparations for his interview with the French King. He spent almost the whole of his time in the company of Prince Henry, narrating to him the thrilling story of the rebellion, and of his wanderings in the Western Highlands. On the Sunday after his arrival at Clichy he drove to Versailles for his state visit to the King. The only distinguishing feature about his dress on this occasion was a white cockade of satin ribbons and diamonds which he wore in his hat. The entire Court was enthusiastic in its reception of the young hero, with whose renown all Europe was filled. Louis saluted him with the words, ' Mon très cher Prince,' embraced him warmly, and in a high-flown speech expressed his ardent wish that so much merit as that possessed by Charles might quickly meet its reward. The Chevalier, however, was unable to persuade his Majesty to assist him to recommence the struggle before the disarming ordered by the Government had taken full effect in the Highlands.

The failure of the late enterprise, while it seemed not to affect the sanguine disposition of Charles, made a deep impression on the mind of the Duke of

York. He was, perhaps, the first of his party to fully recognise in the Battle of Culloden, if not the total extinction of the Stuart hopes, at least the postponement for an indefinite length of time of any fresh attempt to seat his family on the throne. His own inclinations had always been towards a life of study and retirement, although the events of the past few months had forced him into the publicity of political life.

It is not then surprising that the Duke of York should now decide upon quitting the secular life, with all its difficulties and dangers, and taking Holy Orders. This resolution he at once proceeded to put into effect. Leaving Paris secretly, he reached Rome on May 25, 1747. A few days after his arrival, it began to be noised abroad that the younger son of the King of England not only meditated embracing the ecclesiastical state, but was about to be elevated to the dignity of the Cardinalate. This rumour was not long in receiving substantial confirmation. On June 30, 1747, the Duke of York received the tonsure, or initiation into the clerical state, from the hands of the Sovereign Pontiff himself, in the Sistine Chapel, in the presence of his father and the Stuart Court. Four days later it was known that His Royal Highness had been created Cardinal Deacon. On the day his elevation was announced, the Duke, conformably to custom, held a reception at the Stuart Palace, where he received the congratulations of the Sacred College, and of the members of the diplomatic body. On the afternoon of the same day he proceeded in state to the Vatican, and received from the Holy Father the red skull-cap and biretta. He held another reception on July 2, to receive further felicitations from the Roman nobility, and the generals of the various Religious Orders. The following morning the Cardinal Duke, wearing the gorgeous robes of his high dignity, went with great pomp to the Sistine chapel, where he took the customary oaths of fidelity to the Apostolic See. Then, kneeling with his face to the altar, he received from the Pontiff the red hat, symbolical of that martyrdom for which the princes of the Church must ever stand prepared. When the last strains of the *Te Deum*, which marked the termination of this solemn ceremony, had died away, His Royal Highness delivered a set oration, in which he expressed his profound gratitude to the Holy Father for the immense honour he had just received, and the deep sense he felt of his own unworthiness of so great a distinction. Pope Benedict, in his reply, which on this occasion partook of the nature of an allocution to the entire body of cardinals present, thanked the Duke for his gracious words, and, after referring to his birth and illustrious descent, took occasion to remind their Eminences that there was nothing unusual in the elevation of a youth of twenty-two to the Sacred College, seeing that the glorious St. Charles Borromeo had been invested with the purple when of the same age as the Duke of York, while the famous Cardinal Peter de Luxembourg received the red hat from Clement VI. when only eighteen.

It may be interesting to recall the fact that the Duke of York was the third Prince of the English blood-royal to be honoured with the sacred purple, the first being Henry Cardinal Beaufort, son of John of Gaunt, and the second the famous Cardinal Pole,

3

grand-nephew of Edward IV., who reconciled our country to the Apostolic See, after its defection under Henry VIII. and Edward VI.

The Cardinalate of itself confers on the recipient the rank and honours of a prince. The Duke of York, however, in consideration of his birth and the claims of his family, was conceded privileges generally allowed only to those Cardinals who belong to dynasties actually reigning. He wore the royal ermine on his mozetta or short scarlet cloak, above the rochet, took precedence immediately after Cardinal Ruffo, Bishop of Ostia, Dean of the Sacred College, and received, without returning, the visits of the princes of the Church and the lay nobility. This piece of etiquette was not at first understood by the nobles, and gave them much annoyance. After his elevation to the Cardinalate, His Royal Highness was accustomed to give receptions every Thursday evening. These receptions were so numerously attended that it sometimes happened that late comers, much to their chagrin, were unable to gain admittance.

The Roman Senate visited the Duke of York in state to offer their congratulations. The felicitations of the Senators were expressed in Latin, in which language the Cardinal suitably replied. Six days later he underwent the ceremony of having his mouth opened and shut in one and the same consistory, a rite symbolical of the fidelity with which the members of the Sacred College ought to keep the secrets of the Church, and received from the hands of the Pope the Cardinalitial sapphire ring, a gem emblematical of the foundations of the Church foreshadowed by

Isaias.* The Prince, on his side, made the usual offering of several hundred crowns for the promotion of the foreign missions. Benedict conferred upon the newly-created Cardinal the Church of Santa Maria in Campitelli, famous for its curious cross of transparent alabaster, and the tomb of the Blessed Father Leonardi, founder of the Congregation of the Mother of God, as his titular church. It may not be superfluous to mention here that the awarding to each Cardinal, on his elevation, of a titular church is a custom that has come down from the first ages, when the cardinals were the parish priests of Rome, charged with the cure of souls.

* ' O poor little one, tossed with tempest, without all comfort, behold I will lay thy stones in order, and will lay thy foundations with sapphires ' (Isaias liv. 11).

PART II.

1747-1769.

THE news of his brother's ecclesiastical honours had been anything but welcome intelligence to Prince Charles, who foresaw that these events would greatly increase the religious prejudices which stood between the Stuarts and the throne of England. Shortly before the red hat was conferred on his younger son, Prince James wrote to Charles Edward, who was then on a visit to his friend the Duke de Bouillon, informing him of the coming event. The letter commences, ' My dearest Carluccio,' and, after narrating the circumstances of the return of the Duke to Rome, and his resolution of abandoning the lay for the ecclesiastical state, thus concludes: ' I am fully convinced of the sincerity and solidity of his vocation; I should think it a resisting of the will of God, and acting directly against my conscience, if I should pretend to constrain him in a matter which so nearly concerns him.'

We can understand to some extent the resentment felt by the young Chevalier against his father and brother. If they had tacitly abandoned all further attempts against the House of Hanover, he most

certainly had not, as the history of his life abundantly
proves. Of his family, he alone thoroughly understood the intense prejudice entertained by the bulk
of the English nation against the Roman Catholic
Church; and here was his very own brother identifying himself with the most exalted rank but one of the
Roman hierarchy, and becoming one of the sworn
councillors of the Pope! During the progress of the
Rebellion much harm had been done the Stuart cause
by the publication of an impudent forgery, which, to
its lasting shame, the English Government caused to
be published as a statement of the Pretender's plans
should the rising prove successful. It purported to
be an intercepted communication from a Father
Graham, Charles's pseudo - confessor, to the Duke
of York, and was, of course, plentifully interlarded
with sentiments and phrases calculated to excite to
the highest pitch the passions of Protestant Englishmen. The young Chevalier was described as ' wearing
constantly about his neck a small medal . . . on one
side of which is impressed his Royal Highness leading
Britannia repentant to kiss the Pope's toe.' His father,
Prince James, was made to repeat the old calumny
that 'no faith ought to be kept with heretics,' and one
of the concluding sentences of this monstrous fabrica-
tion promised that, should the Stuarts be restored,
' our Smithfield fires shall again blaze !'*

Charles Edward was not the only person who
looked with disfavour on what had lately occurred.
A letter written by Marshal Keith to his brother

* This letter was published by Mr. Cooper, of Paternoster
Row, at the instigation of the Government (1745). Its spurious-
ness is proved by a correspondent in *Notes and Queries* for
June 23, 1855.

about this time expresses the opinion of one of the leading Jacobites on the subject. After referring to the general state of the Stuart affairs, Keith continues: 'Mine are not a bit mended. I have never had one word from C. Smith' (Charles Edward) . . . 'their' (*i.e.*, the Stuarts') 'unfortunate and obstinate choice of favourites and confidants hitherto, particularly of Murray and the Red Cap at Rome, has brought their affairs to such a pitch of discredit that they are under necessity of something to soothe folks,' etc. The Murray alluded to here is Mr. James Murray of Broughton, who acted as secretary to the Chevalier in the year '45, and afterwards saved his own life by turning King's evidence. The 'Red Cap' is, of course, the Cardinal Duke.

Yet another cause of mortification awaited Charles Edward. He had at first hoped that the Cardinalate, being but a princely rank and not a sacred Order, would be no obstacle to his brother marrying at some future time. But on this point, too, he was doomed to disappointment. In August of the same year it was notified to him by Cardinal Valenti that Prince Henry, in accordance with his own wishes and those of the Pope, had resolved on taking Holy Orders. On the 27th of the same month the Duke of York received the four minor Orders from the hands of the Holy Father in the Sistine Chapel, his father being present, with his Court, at the ceremony.

On August 18 following he received the Order of Subdeacon, and a week later that of Deacon, the ceremony of Ordination being performed by the Pope.

On September 1 the Duke was ordained priest, and four days later his Royal Highness said his first Mass in his father's domestic chapel, and administered Holy Communion to his father and several members of the Court. Twelve days afterwards Benedict XIV. created him Cardinal-Priest, but allowed him to retain *in commendam* his diaconal church. On the feast of the Holy Innocents the Cardinal Duke celebrated his first *Missa Cantata,* or sung Mass, in the Sistine Chapel, in the presence of his father and no fewer than twenty-four Cardinals. He was likewise the celebrant at the High Mass sung at St. Peter's on the feast of St. Peter's Chair, January 18, 1749. The function was rendered unusually solemn by the attendance of twenty-two Cardinals in their *cappa magnas,* or long scarlet trains.

In addition to the income allowed his son by Prince James, the Holy Father conferred on the Cardinal Duke the lucrative office and title of Archpriest of the Basilica of St. Peter's. It may not be out of place to remark that the Church of St. Peter's at Rome, from its vast size, calls for the service of a special body of clergy, who are attached to it much in the same way as priests elsewhere are attached to a diocese. As a matter of fact, the Basilica is under the immediate jurisdiction of a bishop, who exercises episcopal authority over all persons in the parish or district adjoining the church.

Shortly after his appointment to this preferment, Cardinal York presented the treasury of St. Peter's with a massive gold chalice of exquisite workmanship, profusely adorned with precious stones of great value. When Rome was plundered by the armies of the French Republic in 1798, this valuable piece of plate fortunately escaped the notice of the modern Vandals, and remains to this day among the treasures of the Vatican, as a memento of the last of the Stuarts and a token of his munificence. As Archpriest of the Basilica, the Cardinal had in his gift several wealthy preferments, that of Vicar of the Basilica being the most considerable.

During the course of the year 1751 Prince James made over to the parochial Church of Santa Maria in Campitelli, the church of his son's cardinalitial title, a sum of money for the purpose of promoting a society which met there every week to recite prayers for the return of Great Britain to the Catholic faith. In accordance with the terms of this gift, to this day thirty candles are lighted on the high altar, and the Blessed Sacrament exposed for adoration, every Saturday one hour before noon. The service consists of a low Mass, during which the Litany of Loretto and the psalm ' Levavi oculos meos in montes ' are chanted, followed by Benediction.

Cardinal York took the liveliest interest in the sodality, and when in Rome never failed to be present at the Saturday devotions, which were attended by a large number of the Roman people, both clerical and lay, and the students of the English, Scotch, and Irish Colleges.

By one of the clauses of the treaty of Aix-la-Chapelle, which was signed in 1748 by the ministers plenipotentiary of England, France, Spain, Holland, and Austria, France pledged herself to expel Charles Edward from her dominions. The Court of St. James's sternly refused to forego this rather petty opportunity for gratifying its vengeance, and the French Government was forced to comply. The difficulty in carrying out this stipulation was that the object of so much diplomatic attention absolutely refused to go. In vain King Louis implored and his father commanded; the young Chevalier remained obdurate, and at last it was found necessary to employ force. As the Prince was stepping out of his carriage one night to enter the Opera, he was seized by six strong sergeants of the Gardes Français, bound hand and foot with a silken cord, and driven to the Bastille. After a short imprisonment in that grim fortress, he was conducted across the frontier, and there set at liberty. To compensate the Stuart family in some degree for this indignity—which, indeed, had been brought entirely on his own head by the Prince himself—and to show his regard for the Cardinal Duke of York, King Louis XV. conferred on his Eminence the rich Abbey of Auchin, in the diocese of Cambray, and four years later that of St. Amand. The possession of these two preferments augmented the Cardinal's already large income by 48,000 Roman crowns or £24,000.

Before his death, which occurred on May 3, 1758, Pope Benedict XIV. gave the Cardinal Duke two further proofs of his appreciation and goodwill. The first of these was the presentation to the Church of the Santi Apostoli, vacant through the death of Cardinal Riviera; and the other the appointment to the office of Camerlengo, which has been well described as the most eminent in all the Court of Rome. The Camerlengo is at the head of the treasury, and during a vacancy of the Papal chair he coins money, issues edicts, and performs other acts of sovereign authority. He has under him a treasurer, an auditor-general, and twelve prelates, called clerks of the Chamber, for the

transaction of minor business. It was not long before
His Royal Highness was called upon to exercise the
very considerable powers with which he was invested.
The Holy Father, as has before been said, expired in
May, 1758, leaving behind him the reputation of
having been the most learned pontiff that ever sat in
St. Peter's chair. Pope Benedict received the tiara
at a time when the infidel spirit of the eighteenth
century had already, in many countries, destroyed
every sentiment of religion in public life, and in
others had made the rulers reluctant to show the Holy
See that respect and deference which the greatest
emperors and potentates of former times had delighted
to manifest to the Vicar of Christ. This state of
things the wise and conciliatory spirit of Benedict XIV.
had in a great measure remedied, while his domestic
enactments were no less conducive to the reform of
abuses and the promotion of prosperity at home. A
foe to religious persecution, he advised the Empress
and other Catholic sovereigns to grant toleration to
their Protestant subjects. During his Pontificate
English, Swedes, and Protestants of other nations
visited Rome in large numbers, and Frederick the
Great and the Czarina Elizabeth consulted him on
many knotty points of State policy. 'He would
make us all Papists if he came to London,' said an
English lord of Benedict on one occasion—a remark
not wholly devoid of truth, since one of the chief
obstacles to the return of Protestants to the ancient
Mother Church is that tangled mass of ignorance
and prejudice concerning her which intercourse with
such men as this immortal Pope would be so eminently
calculated to dispel.

As soon as the Holy Father had expired, Cardinal York, as Camerlengo, wearing his mourning-robes of violet, entered the death-chamber, and remained for some time engaged in prayer with the rest of the prelates present. He then removed the white veil from the face of the Pontiff with the words, 'The Pope is indeed dead,' and after breaking, according to ancient custom, the ring of the Fisherman with a golden hammer, took formal possession of the Vatican, in the name of the Sacred College. This ceremony was followed by the customary despatch of troops to secure the gates of the city and the Castle of St. Angelo, after which the Cardinal Duke returned to his palace, accompanied by the Swiss Guards who usually attend the person of the reigning Pontiff.

The Conclave which assembled on the death of Benedict XIV. was of considerable duration, commencing early in March, and concluding on July 6 with the election of Cardinal Charles Rezzonico, Bishop of Padua, a prelate of great piety and considerable learning, to the vacant throne. The new Pope, who assumed the name of Clement XIII., was crowned at St. Peter's on July 16, in the presence of a concourse remarkable for the great number of English nobility and gentry it contained; for the enlightened rule of the late Pontiff had made Rome the most popular city of resort in Europe.

The election of Clement marked a new era in the ecclesiastical life of Cardinal York. As a prelude to appointing him to one of the metropolitan Sees of Rome, the Pontiff, at a private consistory held on October 2, 1758, nominated him Archbishop of Corinth *in partibus infidelium*. The ceremony of consecration took place in the Cardinal's titular Church of the Santi Apostoli on Sunday, November 19, the Pope himself officiating, assisted by Cardinal Guadagni, Bishop of Porto, and Cardinal Borghese, Bishop of Albano. At the conclusion of the consecration, his Holiness entertained the newly-created Bishop at a grand banquet in the Palazzo Apostolico. On February 12, 1759, Cardinal York renounced his 'title' of Santa Maria in Campitelli, taking in its place that of Santa Maria in Trastevere, retaining, however, *in commendam* the Church of the Santi Apostoli. At the same time, he resigned into the hands of the Sovereign Pontiff the purse of the Camerlengo which he had received from Benedict XIV., whereupon Clement restored it to him with a fresh confirmation of his jurisdiction and powers. Shortly before his consecration as Archbishop of Corinth, a temporary estrangement took place between the Cardinal and his father, the precise cause of which has never been fully explained. It seems, however, that Prince James entertained a strong dislike for a certain Abbé John Lercari, a member of the 'Pious Schools,' and afterwards Archbishop of Genoa, whom the Cardinal, his son, had taken into his household in quality of *Maestro di Camera*, or Chamberlain. The 'King' requested the Cardinal to dismiss Lercari, but the Cardinal, though always most dutiful and affectionate towards his father, felt compelled on this occasion to refuse compliance. To give his father's displeasure time to blow over, his Eminence went for a short visit to Bologna, but fearing that what was in itself only a trifling affair should appear to strangers more serious than it was, he thought it best to return to Rome and dismiss the obnoxious Chamberlain. By the Cardinal's influence, Lercari was promoted to the titular See of Adrianople, and finally, in 1767, translated to the Archdiocese of Genoa, which he ruled till his death in 1802.

In 1761 Cardinal Camillus Paolucci, who since 1758 had filled the See of Frascati, was created Subdean of the Sacred College, an honour which, by long-established custom, necessitated his translation to the See of Porto and Santa Ruffina. On July 13 the Sovereign Pontiff nominated the Cardinal Duke of York as successor to Cardinal Paolucci. In the Consistory held a few days later, His Royal Highness formally renounced the title of Archbishop of Corinth, and took the oath of canonical obedience to the Apostolic See for the Bishopric of Frascati. He likewise renounced his *commendam* of the Church of the Apostoli, but retained that of Santa Maria in Trastevere.

On Wednesday, July 15, the 'Litteræ Confirmationis,' or Bulls of enthronement, of the new Bishop, were read in the Cathedral Church of Frascati by the provost of the Chapter, and on the Saturday following the Cardinal took up his residence in the episcopal palace. The town of Frascati, which for upwards of forty years was to be associated with the last of the Stuarts, is a comparatively modern superstructure erected on an ancient site, having sprung up during the middle ages among the ruins of the old Roman city of Tusculum. The name is said to be derived from Frascata, which, as far back as the eighth century, was given to the locality on account of its woody appearance. Its environs now, as in ancient times, are renowned for the number and beauty of the villas which dot the country ; but the town itself has few buildings of interest beyond a fountain constructed in 1480 by Cardinal d'Estouteville, and the cathedral, with its curious imitation dome above the sanctuary.

At the time of his translation to Frascati, the Cardinal Duke acquired the Villa Muti Savorelli, beautifully situated at the foot of the hill, and at a short distance from the fountain of Vermicino. Mr. George Stillman Hillard, the American traveller, who visited it in 1853, describes it as an unpretentious though well-arranged building, containing ' a large number of immense rooms generally opening into each other. . . . Many of the floors are paved with tiles or brick, like the hearth of a country farmhouse.' Up to this time the Cardinal had occupied a portion of his father's palace, but upon his appointment to the Bishopric of Frascati, he caused his household and effects to be removed to Frascati. Here he formed the splendid collection of historic and art treasures which, till the time of their dispersion·at the Revolution, made the Cardinal's episcopal residence one of the show-places of Italy.

On Sunday, July 19, the day after his arrival, Cardinal York took possession solemnly and publicly of his See, and pontificated at the High Mass which followed this function. The Cathedral was crowded with the élite of Rome, several of the British and foreign nobility being also present, as well as Prince James, who, as 'King of England,' occupied a throne on the right of the sanctuary. To testify their joy at the accession of the Prince-Bishop, the inhabitants of

the town and vicinity celebrated the event by bonfires
and illuminations. His Royal Highness, on his part,
entertained the Cathedral Chapter and principal
personages of the place at a grand banquet, while
among the poor of the neighbourhood clothes, money,
and other necessaries were distributed in large
quantities. He likewise presented the Cathedral with
two rich Planetas or folded chasubles for use during
Lent and Advent. On Thursday, July 23, his Eminence
gave Confirmation to more than eighty boys and girls
in the Cathedral, and on the evening of the same day
returned to Rome.

The Cardinal had not long been translated to the
See of Frascati when he manifested his zeal by two
much-needed undertakings. One was the complete
reorganization of the diocesan seminary; the other
the promulgation of a number of salutary laws for the
better government of the clergy of the diocese. Early
in 1763 orders were issued for the convocation of a
Synod, which met at Frascati on May 8, and terminated
on May 11 of the same year. The synodal decrees
were subsequently published in two bulky quartos
under the direction of the Vicar-General, Father
Stefanucci, S.J. The title-pages of this work, which
was printed in Latin and Italian, bear his Eminence's
armorial device, the royal arms of England, surmounted
by the Cardinal's hat, and supported on either side
by angelic heralds. The work commences with a
Latin address to the Cardinal Bishops of the six
metropolitan Sees of Rome.

The statutes dealing with the discipline of the
clergy may be passed over without notice, as they
contain merely a repetition of what had been repeatedly

enforced in all dioceses since the time of the holy
Council of Trent. It was with the reconstruction of
his seminary, to which the flock committed to his care
had to look for a supply of zealous pastors, that the
Cardinal was chiefly concerned. This institution,
which had been founded about the middle of the
sixteenth century, by Cardinal Cesi, had fallen into
a state of great decay, so that its immediate recon-
stitution was a matter of the first importance. The
Cardinal Bishop rebuilt at his own expense that fabric
itself, in a style suited to the requirements for which
the institution was intended. The site chosen for the
new building was among the vineyards of that de-
lightful locality where tradition says the martial
sybarite Lucullus had his country residence, near the
Villa Montalto, now the property of the Propaganda.

A series of stringent regulations were drawn up,
with the approbation of the Cardinal, for the government of the new institution. The students, as far as
possible, were to be natives of the diocese, and, thanks
to the bounty of his Eminence, those who could not
afford the moderate annual fees were maintained on
a number of free bursaries, founded by himself. The
course of studies pursued at the seminary occupied
nine years, arranged in the following order: First, two
years of Greek and Latin grammar, followed by two
years of the classical authors, both prose and verse,
with modern history and literature. Then came the
Ecclesiastical studies proper, commencing with Philosophy, which lasted a year. To Philosophy succeeded
four years' study of Dogmatic and Moral Theology,
Scripture and Canon Law. Cardinal York was careful
to make due provision for the instruction of the

students in Gregorian chants and liturgical ceremonies, in which last branch they were to be exercised twice a week in the Cathedral by a Magister Ceremoniarum appointed for the purpose, and paid at the rate of two scudi a lesson.

The Cardinal gave the entire management of the seminary to the Jesuits, as the body most fitted by learning and experience in spiritual training for the direction of aspirants to the sacred priesthood. The rector was his Eminence's confessor and Vicar-General, Father Horatius Steffanucci, of whom mention has been made. This remarkable man had entered the Society of Jesus at the age of nineteen, and, after completing the long and arduous course of study prescribed by the rule of St. Ignatius, and receiving priest's Orders, was appointed Professor of Canon Law at the German College in Rome, a post he held for twenty-five years. Cardinal York became acquainted with him through a mutual friend, the famous Cardinal John Francis Albani, and so impressed was his Royal Highness with Father Steffanucci's learning and capacity for business, that he made him his Vicar-General, and consulted him on all matters pertaining to the welfare of the diocese.

Of the many ecclesiastical students who afterwards rose to eminence, either as Churchmen or scholars, thanks in great measure to the patronage of Cardinal York, two deserve an especial mention. The first of these was the immortal Cardinal Consalvi, whose diplomatic ability, as manifested in the conflict between the Holy See and the French Empire, won for him from Napoleon the title of the 'Siren of Rome.'

The young Consalvi, shortly after the death of the

4

Marquis, his father, in 1763, was sent with his brother
to the seminary of Frascati, by his guardian, Cardinal
Andrew Negroni, who for several years filled the high
judicial post of Auditor-General under Cardinal York.
After completing his studies at the seminary, and
taking his degree in Canon Law at the University
with great applause, the young Consalvi entered upon
that diplomatic career which was to win for him the
honours of the Roman purple, and engage him in one
of the most terrible struggles in the field of politics
that the world has ever seen.

Another protégé of the Cardinal Duke's who afterwards obtained considerable reputation in public life
was Thomas Erskine, subsequently Cardinal and
envoy of Pope Pius VI. to the Court of George III.
His father was Colin, son of Sir Alexander Erskine,
Bart., who lived and died in Rome, an exile for the
Stuart cause.   Young Erskine, being early left an
orphan, was placed by his Eminence in the Scots'
College, in Rome, an institution which was ever regarded with peculiar veneration and affection by
Cardinal York.   After a long and distinguished
career, spent in the service of the Holy See, Monsignor Erskine was, in January 1803, proclaimed
Cardinal Deacon of the Church of Santa Maria in
Campitelli, an honour which contained a special
reference to his friend and patron the Cardinal Duke
of York, who had formerly held the 'title.'   His
death occurred at Paris on March 20, 1811, caused, it
is said, by grief at the deplorable persecution which
the Sovereign Pontiff, whom he had accompanied to
France, was then enduring at the hands of the French
Emperor.

In the summer of 1765 it became apparent to all who knew him that Prince James, the Cardinal's father, had not long to live. The Prince had, indeed, been in declining health for several years, and in consideration of his age and infirmities had, like Charles V., been dispensed by the Pope from fasting before receiving Holy Communion. As the autumn wore on to winter the old Chevalier kept himself very much to his palace, saw few visitors, and beyond an occasional visit of state to the Vatican, seldom went out. His domestic and other affairs were attended to by Cardinal York and a Mr. Graham, on whom James had conferred the title of Lord Alford. By December James was confined to his bed, and in anticipation of his approaching end, asked that an altar might be erected in his apartment, so that Mass might be said daily in his presence, either by one of his chaplains, or by the Cardinal, who was constantly at his father's bedside. On Christmas-day the Holy Viaticum was administered to the dying Prince, who rapidly grew worse, till on the afternoon of January 1, 1766, his death was momentarily expected. The entire household was summoned to the sick-room, where the prayers for the dying were recited by the Cardinal, while prayers for the same intention were offered up by the students of the English, Scotch, and Irish Colleges, and at most of the churches in Rome. Shortly before midnight James ceased to breathe, and, upon examination, the physicians pronounced life to be extinct. The obsequies accorded the deceased Prince were the same as those for a monarch that had actually reigned. After the embalmment the body was attired in royal robes, and lay in state for five

days in the apartment where the death had occurred.
This apartment, in accordance with the prevailing
custom, was transformed into a *chapelle ardente,*
adorned with rich hangings and armorial bearings,
and lighted with large candles of yellow wax set in
great candlesticks of massive silver. On January 6
the corpse was taken to the Church of the Santi
Apostoli, accompanied by the chief officials of the
Papal household, the Roman nobility, and representatives of all the religious Orders and confraternities in
Rome. A thousand wax candles and funereal torches
blazed round the catafalque, and twenty violet-robed
Cardinals supported the pall. On its arrival at the
church the body was removed to a bed of state
surrounded by purple hangings and gold lace. The
canopy was surmounted by figures of angels sup-
porting the crown and sceptre of England, while
beneath ran the inscription 'Jacobus Magnæ Britan-
niæ Rex, Anno MDCCLXVI.,' surrounded by medallions
emblazoned with devices of the English orders of
chivalry. In accordance with the ghastly fashion of
the time, the sepulchral appearance of the church
was intensified by the use of a number of bronze
effigies of Death holding candelabra. Mass was
celebrated by his Eminence Cardinal Alberoni,
nephew of the famous minister, while the musical
portions of the requiem were chanted by the choir of
the Apostolic College. Masses for the repose of the
King's soul were also offered up by Cardinal York at
the churches of the Apostoli and Santa Maria in
Trastevere, as well as by the dean of the cathedral at
Frascati, and the chaplains of the British Colleges in
Rome. Three days after the conclusion of the

obsequies, the remains of the deceased Prince were removed to St. Peter's and deposited in the vault prepared for their interment.

Of the private fortune left by the Chevalier the great bulk naturally went to Prince Charles, the Cardinal being already amply provided for by his rich benefices in Italy and France. In money alone the fortune of the deceased amounted to over £200,000, while it also included the Crown jewels of England which King James II. had taken with him on his flight in 1688, and the magnificent collection of plate and jewels, estimated at nearly a million of money, which had formed part of the dowry of the Princess Maria Clementina. These latter included a large shield of pure gold that had been given by the Emperor to John Sobieski, after one of the latter's signal victories over the Turks, and some immense rubies taken by the same illustrious conqueror from his Moslem foe.

After the death of James the Holy See declined to recognise the right of the Stuarts to the title of King. Prudence, as well as political expediency, demanded that Charles, James's heir, should be regarded as of princely, but not sovereign, rank ; for by identifying itself with the cause of the exiled family, the Pontifical Government was giving to the Court of St. James's a very strong pretext for continuing the penal laws against its Catholic subjects, on the ground that they obeyed a power that lent its authority and prestige for the purpose of advancing the claims of a pretender. Cardinal York, as was only to be expected, warmly espoused the cause of his brother, who was absent from Rome at the time the above decision was arrived at, and, in an interview with the Pontiff, implored him to reconsider the resolution he had taken. The French Ambassador, M. d'Aubeterre, joined his solicitations to those of the Cardinal, but all that these representations could elicit from Clement was a promise to consult the Sacred College before proceeding further in the matter. The result of this consultation was that the Senate of the Church, with almost unanimous voice, approved of the policy of rejecting the claim of Charles Edward to be recognised as Charles III. The repudiation of these pretensions to the British throne involved the deprivation of the right to nominate to vacant bishoprics in Ireland, which ever since the Revolution had been enjoyed by the Stuarts, and was now transferred to the Congregation of Propaganda.

When Charles arrived in Rome, no notice was taken of his presence by the authorities, nor did any of the Cardinals visit him. To console his brother for this cold reception, Cardinal York took special care to show him all the honour in his power. He several times visited the Chevalier in state, addressed him in public as 'your majesty,' and in driving out with him in Rome, placed him on his right hand—an honour shown by Cardinals only to reigning sovereigns. The immediate friends of the Cardinal soon followed suit. Cardinal Orsini, Neapolitan Minister in Rome, attended all Charles's receptions, and gave him homage as a King, as also did the priors of the Orders of Malta, Altieri, and Fiano, and the rectors of the English, Scotch, and Irish Colleges. This public defiance of the law drew from the Government a circular of stern reprimand, while the rectors of the

British Colleges, as born subjects of King George, and therefore more likely to attract the displeasure of their Government by an act which at home would be reckoned high treason, were banished for some time from Rome.

Prince Charles was already beginning to succumb to those confirmed habits of intemperance which have cast so deep a gloom over his memory. To distract his attention from the mortifications he had lately suffered, Cardinal York, in the autumn of 1766, invited his brother to Frascati for the shooting season. The Prince, who was still as keen a sportsman and as good a shot as when he brought down partridges in the Isle of Skye, remained in the country till the end of the season, residing alternately at Frascati with the Cardinal and at his own hunting lodge near Albano.

In a drinking bout one evening at this latter place he drew his sword on one of the company, and, but for the intervention of those present, history might have had to lay homicide to the charge of the young Chevalier. Writing to a friend concerning this unhappy incident, the Cardinal remarked :

' I have very little to say except to deplore the continuance of the bottle ; that, I own to you, makes me despair of everything, and I am of opinion that it is impossible for my brother to live if he continues in this strain. You say he ought to be sensible of all I have endeavoured to do for his good ; whether he is or not is more than I can tell, for he has never said anything of that kind to me. What is certain is, that he has a singular tenderness and regard for me and all that regards myself, and as singular an inflexibility and disregard for everything that regards his own good. I am seriously afflicted on his account, when I reflect on the dismal situation he puts himself under, which is a thousand times worse than the situation his enemies have endeavoured to place him in; but there is no remedy except a miracle, which may be kept at last for his eternal salvation, but surely nothing else.'

The miserable effects of intemperance, as exemplified in his own brother, induced the Cardinal to draw up his well-known paper on the 'Sins of the Drunkard' for distribution among the clergy and faithful of his diocese. It is a complete summary of the Catholic doctrine on the subject, and has been since translated into several languages. In England at the present day it forms the substance of the temperance resolutions directed to be read in every church and chapel of the Catholic diocese of Liverpool on the first Sunday of February and July.

When once the Pope had clearly manifested his resolution of refusing sovereign honours to the Stuarts, no one more readily submitted to the will of the Pontiff than Cardinal York himself. In conjunction with some of his friends, he now urged his brother to lay aside the empty title of Charles III. for that of Count of Albany, which would be granted to him readily by everyone. This title was intimately connected with the Royal House of Stuart, having been first bestowed in 1398 on Robert Stuart, second son of Robert II., King of Scotland. The dukedom afterwards passed to the famous John Stuart, who was Regent during the minority of James V., son of the king who fell at Flodden Field. It finally descended to Henry Darnley, the ill-starred husband of Mary Queen of Scots. Moreover, James II., Charles's grandfather, before ascending the throne, had borne the title of Duke of York and Albany.

The advice of the Cardinal was assuredly well-timed, if we are to judge of Charles's relations with society at this time, as given in the following letter from Sir William Hamilton, our ambassador at Naples, to Lord Shelburne, dated May, 1767. This communication is interesting also from the insight it gives into Cardinal York's acts of benevolence. It proceeds thus:

'The Pretender is hardly thought of even at Rome. The life he leads is now very regular and sober; his chief occupation is shooting in the environs of Rome, and the only people he can see and converse with are his few attendants, Messrs. Lumsden, Montgomery, etc. The pension his father had of £1,200 a year from the Court of Rome is now granted to the Cardinal; but, as he was not in the least want of any addition to his income, he gives it to the present Pretender, and, it is said, allows him £1,800 more out of his own income. The Cardinal's ecclesiastical benefices in the Roman States and in France are said to amount to £18,000 a year, with which he does much good, being extremely generous. Besides the £3,000 he allows the Pretender, he is supposed to give at least £2,000 more in private donations to support poor families at Rome. The Father left a considerable quantity of jewels to the present Pretender, which still remain untouched.'*

* The annual income of the Cardinal at this time could not have been less than £40,000 a year, for the Court of Spain had recently made over to him some very rich estates (or benefices) in Mexico.

Convinced at length of the necessity of complying, Charles fell in with these overtures, and, as a pledge of his sincerity in submitting to the Pope's wishes, expressed his intention of visiting the Pontiff, in company with Cardinal York.

When the time appointed for the interview arrived, the Cardinal drove his brother in his state coach to the Vatican, and, in accordance with his privilege as a Prince of the Church, was immediately admitted into the presence of the Pontiff. Charles, who had remained seated in an ante-room, was, after some little delay, summoned to the audience by one of the chamberlains, who addressed him merely as the brother of Cardinal York. On entering the Pope's private apartment, the Chevalier kissed his Holiness's hand, and remained kneeling like any other visitor till desired to rise. During the whole visit, which lasted a quarter of an hour, Charles stood, although his brother, like the Pope, remained seated.

Having shown his goodwill by complying with the wishes of the Head of the Church, the Chevalier became a *persona grata* at the Vatican, and at the same time resumed the place he had lost in society. On the occasion of one of his visits to Clement XIII., the Holy Father presented him with a rosary of gold and precious stones, of the sort usually given only to reigning princes, and, it is said, informed him at the same time that political considerations alone prevented the Government from giving him the honours due to kingly rank.

Some notice must now be taken of the political events which at this time were giving to the Holy See such serious grounds for alarm. The peace and tranquillity enjoyed by the States of the Church during the glorious reign of Benedict XIV. terminated with the death of that Pontiff, and the tiara had scarcely descended to his successor when the long-expected storm burst with incredible fury. The cause of this tempest in the religious and political firmament was the corporate existence of the Jesuits.

In the third quarter of the eighteenth century the Society of Jesus, though it had lost much of its former prestige and influence, was still by far the most potent religious community in the Church. Its members laboured for the conversion of the heathen and ignorant beneath the sun of India and amidst the snow-bound regions of the North. Its schools were largely frequented by scholars of all classes, and its reputation for learning in every department of knowledge was still well maintained. But its enemies were numerous and powerful. France, Spain, and Portugal were the countries in which opposition to the Society was the strongest; for, though outwardly Catholic, these nations, especially France, had drunk deeply of the waters of infidelity and moral corruption which at this miserable epoch threatened to destroy the very foundations of religious and social life. The opinion of French philosophic atheism was well expressed by Voltaire when he wrote: 'Once we have exterminated the Jesuits, the destruction of that infamous thing (*i.e.*, Christianity) will be only child's play for us.'

The French Episcopate, to its everlasting credit, did its utmost to defend the Jesuits, but in vain. By 1764 the royal decrees against the Fathers had been everywhere enforced, and the Society no longer existed in France. The Jesuits had already been expelled from Portugal, and a little later they were expelled from Spain.

It was not to be expected that the Sovereign Pontiff could witness these savage aggressions without raising his voice in solemn protest. His Bulls and edicts commanding the restoration of the Society in France were, however, not likely to produce much effect in a country where religion had almost entirely disappeared beneath the most bestial immorality and blatant infidelity. Clement convoked a Consistory for January 3, 1769, to consider the dangers threatening the Church; but ere it could assemble, the soul of the sorely-tried Pontiff had passed away.

The remains of the deceased Pope were deposited in St. Peter's, beneath a monument representing Death and Religion in an attitude of meditation, a monument which has excited the admiration of generations of visitors to the Eternal City. Never, perhaps, in the whole history of the Church did a Conclave assemble in such momentous circumstances as that which met after the death of Clement XIII. The so-called Catholic Powers—France, Spain and Portugal—informed the Cardinals that no Pontiff would be acceptable who was not pledged to abolish the Society of Jesus. Such a declaration as this portended a schism in the already distracted Church, the avoidance of which was the problem imperatively calling for solution.

On February 15, 1769, the Cardinals, at the conclusion of the Mass of the Holy Ghost, entered the Conclave in procession, shortly after mid-day, and at once entered upon the business of the election. From the outset the Conclave was divided into two sections

—the Cardinals who favoured the demands of the Bourbon Kings, and the Cardinals who defended the corporate existence of the Jesuits. Among the former party were numbered the Cardinals York, Orsini, Conti, Corsini, Cavalchini, and Carraccioli. The latter party, however, outnumbered its opponents at the outset by more than three-fourths. An attempt was made by the Cardinals Rezzonico and Albani, the leading supporters of the Jesuits, to complete the election before the arrival of the Cardinals from the Bourbon Courts who were on their way to Rome. But the suggestion of hasty procedure in a matter of such grave importance met with almost general condemnation. In a conference held on February 19 between the Cardinals York, Lanti, Rezzonico and Perelli, it was clearly demonstrated that such a course, far from restoring peace to the Spouse of Christ, would be productive of nothing but calamities. The election consequently assumed its normal aspect, and so continued till an event occurred which for a time diverted the attention of the august assembly. This was the arrival in Rome on March 15 of Joseph II. of Austria and his brother Leopold, Duke of Tuscany. Two days later the imperial visitors attended a session of the Conclave. Though the visitors maintained the strictest incognito, the Cardinals did not fail to honour their illustrious guests with an imposing display of pomp and splendour.* The Cardinals Albani, Orsini

* The state robes of a Cardinal are splendid, consisting of a scarlet silk cassock, lace rochet, short red silk cloak, or long cape (*mozetta*), and *cappa magna;* an ample train of scarlet silk, twelve yards long, fastened to the shoulders by a rich hood of silk or ermine, according to season. The famous red hat, with its pendant tassels, is seldom or never worn, its place being

and Spinola received the Emperor and his brother, and presented to them the Florentine and Milanese Cardinals as being their immediate subjects. The visitors then withdrew to the Sistine Chapel, where they adored the Blessed Sacrament, which was exposed for their veneration, after which they returned to the main hall of the Conclave, and engaged in familiar conversation with various members of the Sacred College. Cardinal York on this occasion became the especial object of the Emperor's attention, for the son of Maria Theresa was not unmindful of the deep debt of gratitude owed by his House to his Eminence's immortal ancestor, John Sobieski, the deliverer of Vienna.

Although the visit of the Emperor took place in Holy Week, none of the imposing ceremonies of the Church proper to that solemn season could be carried out, owing to the vacancy in the Papal throne. But by order of Cardinal York, as Camerlengo, the great dome of St. Peter's was illuminated with countless lamps on the evening of Easter Monday, and the entire week following was spent in festivals and rejoicings. The Roman nobility vied with each other in showing honour to the heir of the Cæsars, and a series of splendid fêtes were given at the magnificent villas of the families of Braciano, Corsini, Albani and Doria. On April 10 the Empress Maria Theresa, the

---

taken by the scarlet biretta. In Lent, and on occasions of mourning, violet robes take the place of the scarlet, and on the first Sunday of Advent rose-colour, though the scarlet zuchetto or skull-cap is worn at all times. Cardinals belonging to the great religious Orders usually retain their monastic habit, but, like the rest of the Sacred College, are distinguished by the zuchetto, sapphire ring and pectoral cross.

mother of Joseph and joint ruler of the Empire with him, addressed an elegantly-worded Latin letter to the Conclave, thanking the Cardinals and the Roman people for the reception given to her sons. The Emperor and his brother had already quitted Rome, but on their return to Vienna, the former despatched an embassy headed by Count Kaunitz-Rittburg, son of the Chancellor of the Empire, to suitably express the profound thanks of the Austrian Court for the honours shown to the person of the Sovereign by the Sacred College. So splendid was the reception given to this embassy by the Cardinals that the French Ambassador, though accustomed to the brilliant ceremonial of Versailles, afterwards described it in a letter as the most magnificent scene he had ever witnessed in the whole course of a long series of courtly pageants.

The Conclave now returned to its task of selecting a Pontiff at once agreeable to the Courts and capable of maintaining in its integrity the prestige of the Apostolic See. In the midst of their deliberations, Monsignor Azparu arrived with the Veto which the Governments of France, Spain and Portugal had drawn up, prohibiting the election of certain Cardinals. The envoy informed Cardinal Orsini that the Powers he represented required that the Pope-elect should give a formal undertaking to suppress the Society of Jesus. Orsini rejected this proposal with indignation, and declared that any attempt of the Civil powers to overstep the lawful provisions of the Veto would cause any election that might come about through such influence to be absolutely null and void. This reply had the desired effect, and no further attempts were made to unduly influence the progress of the Conclave.

It would be tedious to follow this protracted election through all its details. We content ourselves with stating that at the last scrutiny, or examination of votes, taken on May 19, Cardinal Ganganelli was found to have united all the suffrages.

The excitement aroused by an assembled Conclave invariably causes the great square outside St. Peter's to be filled both day and night with a dense crowd eager to witness the pulling down of the walled-up window that marks the coming of the Senior Cardinal to announce the name and title of the new occupant of the Papal throne. The great length of the Conclave on the present occasion had the effect of lessening the popular interest, and it was not the voice of a Cardinal, but the boom of the guns from the heights of St. Angelo, that first announced to the city that a new Pope had been elected.

PART III.

1769—1807.

OHN VINCENT ANTHONY GANGANELLI, who, after so long an interval, was summoned to the headship of the Church, under the name of Clement XIV., was already known throughout Italy for his extensive learning, unaffected piety, and cheerfulness of disposition. Born in 1705, at St. Arcangelo, near Rimini, he had, on the completion of his studies, entered the Franciscan Order, where his uncommon ability led his superiors to appoint him professor of philosophy and theology. His elucidation of the works of the great luminary of his Order, Duns Scotus, procured for him an extraordinary reputation, and on September 24, 1759, he was proclaimed a Cardinal by Clement XIII. His promotion wrought no change in his conduct. His friends missed nothing of his wonted cheerfulness, while strangers, instead of the dignified reserve of the Roman prince, saw nothing in him but a monk filled with humility.

The coronation of the Pope-elect passed off amidst the customary splendour. The ceremony of Episcopal consecration was performed by his Eminence Cardinal Cavalchini-Guidobono, Bishop of Ostia, while the

coronation service was performed by the youngest
Cardinal Deacon *in curia*. Cardinal York, as Archpriest of the Basilica, addressed the Holy Father in a
Latin oration, on behalf of himself and the Chapter of
St. Peter's, during the course of which his Royal
Highness referred, with a singular happiness of
expression, to the glorious succession of Pontiffs
who, like the object of his congratulation, bore the
name that told of mildness and mercy.

Though the accession of Clement XIV. was received with signs of apparent approval by the various
European Powers, it may be doubted if any Pontiff
ever succeeded to the Chair of St. Peter under darker
auspices. The Courts of France and Spain were
clamouring for the immediate suppression of the
Jesuits, Portugal was seriously thinking of setting
up an independent patriarch, while the Republic of
Venice, emboldened by these examples, was passing
several *senatus-consulta* highly prejudicial to the
interests of the Church and the Holy See. In
Asia Minor the Christian communities about Mount
Lebanon who acknowledged the primacy of the
Roman Pontiff were enduring a violent persecution
from the Turks and Russians. This formidable array
of dangers did not dismay the Pope. Assured, as
every Catholic must always be, of the ultimate
triumph of the Church whose glorious Spouse, the
Saviour of the world, abides with her for ever, he
calmly faced the situation. He appointed Cardinal
Pallavicini, a consummate diplomatist, his Secretary
of State, raised the Cardinal Duke of York to the
office of Vice-Chancellor of the Apostolic See, despatched Monsignor Martorelli, Archbishop of Sidon,

as Nuncio to arrange matters with the Government of
Venice, addressed a letter to the pious Empress Maria
Theresa, requesting her to use her influence with the
Czar and Sultan on behalf of the Eastern Christians,
and finally informed the Bourbon Courts that their
demands should be submitted to the investigation of
a committee of Cardinals and Canonists.

Early in 1770 the Pope promulgated a constitution
which caused the utmost excitement in Rome. This
was nothing less than the dismissal of the Jesuits
from the seminary of Frascati, and the placing of that
institution under secular priests. Cardinal York, as
Bishop of the diocese, incurred a good deal of un-
merited odium at the time for his supposed over-
zealousness in carrying out the Pontifical ordinance,
as we learn from the following letter written by
Father Galloway, S.J., to Father Thomas Hawkins,
Chaplain at Oxburgh Hall, Lancashire :

' Bad news from Rome. Cardinal York has seized
on the college and church at Frascati, with all the
effects, movable and immovable, and the Brief
mentions no other reason than his zeal and desire
of having it. Visitations are going on, as in
Henry VIII.'s time, and the consequence is seizure.
The visit of the Roman College is postponed by
reason of Cardinals Negroni and Pisani refusing to
act in conjunction with Cardinal Marefoschi.'

The ' zeal and desire' of Cardinal York to possess
the property of the Jesuits connected with the church
and seminary at Frascati may have arisen from a fear
of its passing into other hands, and so being lost to
the college ; or it may well be that much of the
property had originally been given to the Society

by himself, and that he was only claiming the
reversion. But whatever his motive may have been,
we may be sure that he was not prompted by avarice,
as the reader will, we doubt not, readily acknowledge
after what has been already said of the kind and
generous disposition of Cardinal York.

We may now leave this painful topic for a time,
to say something of the marriage of Prince Charles
Edward, which took place in the spring of 1772.

As it was the policy of France to perpetuate the
House of Stuart, and thus have ever at hand a ready
means of disquieting her great rival, England, the
Duke d'Aguillon, the French Minister of State,
intimated to Charles, through his cousin, the Duke
de FitzJames, in the summer of 1771, the strong
desire felt by the Court of Versailles to see him
married. The Chevalier thereupon proceeded to
Paris, and, after several interviews with the Minister,
agreed to unite himself in marriage with any eligible
bride that might be selected, on condition of receiving
a pension of £10,000 a year.

After a considerable amount of further negotiation,
an 'eligible bride' was found in the person of the
Princess Louise, daughter of Prince Gustavus of
Stolberg-Gerden, a brave cavalry officer, who fell
at the Battle of Leuthen in the Seven Years' War.
Her maternal grandfather was Thomas Bruce, second
Earl of Aylesbury, and a noted Jacobite, while her
sister, the Princess Caroline, was betrothed to the
eldest son of the Duke de FitzJames, who, as most
of our readers are aware, was the direct descendant
of James II.

The preliminaries being at length concluded, the

Chevalier and his bride were married by proxy at
Paris on March 28, 1772. The actual celebration
took place twenty-one days later in the chapel
attached to the villa of Cardinal Campagnoni-Mare-
foschi at Macerata, in the marches of Ancona.
Charles wore on this occasion a suit of crimson
silk, and as insignia the ribbon and star of the
Garter. He signed his name in the register as
'Charles III., King of Great Britain, France, and
Ireland, 1772,' while the bride added to her name
the title of Queen.

On the Wednesday of Easter week their Royal
Highnesses set out for Rome. They were met near
the city by Cardinal York, accompanied by his state
coaches and his retinue in scarlet and gold. The
streets of Rome leading to the Stuart palace were
lined with people, eager to see Charles and his
consort; but otherwise no notice was taken of their
arrival, although a formal intimation of the same
had been made to the Cardinal Secretary of State.

On the day following his brother's entry into Rome,
Cardinal York, who, in quality of Archpriest of the
Vatican Basilica, was residing in the palace in the
piazza behind St. Peter's, made his sister-in-law a
morning call, and presented her with a truly princely
wedding present, consisting of a beautifully wrought
box of embossed gold, set with brilliants. When
opened, the precious casket was found to contain a
draft on his Eminence's bankers for 20,000 Roman
crowns, or about £10,000.

Another royal visitor arrived in Rome at this time
in the person of William, Duke of Gloucester, brother
of King George III. The Duke received a magnificent

reception from the Papal Government, and had several private interviews with the Pope, who was glad of this opportunity for speaking to his Royal Highness on the deplorable condition of the Catholics in the British Isles. The Duke, whose goodness of heart and liberality of sentiment were well known, needed no reminder to make him aware of the cruelty and injustice of the penal laws which weighed so heavily on so large a number of his fellow-subjects, and on his return to England exerted himself in such a manner with the Government as to pave the way for the first Catholic Relief Act, which became law some years later.

Not long after the departure of his distant cousin, the Duke of Gloucester, who, while in Rome, frequently expressed his deep commiseration for the misfortunes of the Stuart family, Cardinal York received information from Scotland of a most cruel persecution which was being carried on against a large number of the Catholic crofters of South Uist by their hereditary laird, Macdonald of Boisdale. This harsh personage offered his wretched tenants the choice of turning Presbyterians or being evicted from their homes. Cardinal York laid an account of this sad state of things before the Pontiff. His Holiness at once communicated with his Eminence Cardinal Roche-Aymon, Grand Almoner and Confessor of King Louis XV., requesting him to draw the attention of the British Government to the conduct of the island despot. It does not appear that any attempt was made to restrain the Presbyterian zeal of Boisdale, for the persecution went on unchecked.

At length Bishop Hay, the Vicar Apostolic of Edinburgh, who, when a young man, had fought

for Prince Charles in 1745, collected a sufficient sum
from the Catholic nobility and gentry of Great Britain
to enable the evicted families to emigrate to America,
where they founded a large and flourishing colony.
The emigrants were accompanied in their exile by
Mr. Macdonald of Glenaladale, the cousin of their
persecutor, and a Catholic, who nobly disposed of
his family estate that he might have the means
of assisting his poor co-religionists who were flying
from the tyranny of his heartless kinsman. There is
reason to believe that the emigration fund so nobly
started by Bishop Hay received substantial contributions from Cardinal York and his brother, both of
whom were on terms of intimacy with the eminent
author of the ' Sincere Christian.'

The death of Clement XIV. took place in the
middle part of the year 1774, about a year after the
promulgation of the famous Brief ' Dominus ac Re-
demptor Noster,' which declared the Society of Jesus
at an end. The suppression of the Jesuits was a
political expedient intended to avert the threatened
schism between the Bourbon countries and the Holy
See. The existence of any religious Order is quite
accidental and contingent, whereas it is absolutely
necessary that the whole Church should be joined in
spiritual communion with the successor of St. Peter.
Clement declared the Society dissolved on the ground
that the altered relations between the Church and the
modern world rendered it undesirable that the Jesuits
should continue to exist as a corporate body. His
predecessors had from time to time suppressed other
religious Orders as unsuited to the altered conditions
of the age.

Such of the Jesuit Fathers as were too old or too infirm to undertake parish work were assigned pensions. It was, however, unfortunately deemed necessary in carrying out the provisions of the Brief to confine the General of the Society, Father Lorenzo Ricci, to the Castle of St. Angelo as a State prisoner. Here he remained in ~~close~~ imprisonment till his death some months later, on November 25, 1775, asserting to the last the entire innocence of his brethren of the offences laid by their enemies to their charge.*

The action of Clement in suppressing the Society of Jesus, and thus appearing to give a quasi endorsement to charges that were never proved, has been much censured by some Catholic historians, who have contrasted the conduct of this Pope with that of Pius IX. In somewhat similar circumstances Pius IX. found a way out of the difficulty arising from the opposition of one of the Governments of Europe to the Jesuits, by advising the Fathers to retire for a time from that particular country.

In Holy Week of 1774 Clement XIV. manifested the first symptoms of his mortal sickness, and in the following July his physicians ordered him to retire to his country residence of Castel Gandolfi. Here he was visited several times by Cardinal York. On October 20 Clement received the Holy Viaticum, and on the following day Extreme Unction, in the presence of Cardinals Malvezzi, Simone, and Negroni, as well as all the Superiors-General of the religious Orders in Rome. Next day at one o'clock in the afternoon Clement XIV. breathed his last, in the seventieth

* The Society of Jesus was subsequently restored by Pope Pius VII. in 1814.

year of his age and sixth of his Pontificate. The Conclave which met to elect his successor, though somewhat protracted in length, presents none of the features which marked the previous Conclave. Cardinal York, who was to share with the future Pontiff the vicissitudes of fortune, acted as Vice-Chancellor of the Apostolic See on this occasion, and in that capacity issued the silver medals for distribution among the prelates and nobility of Rome as passports to certain parts of the Vatican palace during the sitting of the Conclave. These medals had on the obverse the arms of his Eminence surmounted by a Cardinal's hat, and on the reverse the inscription: 'Henricus Cardinalis Dux. Ebor. S.R.E. Vicecancellarius Sede. vacan. 1774.' [Henry, Cardinal of the Holy Roman Church, Duke of York, and Vice-Chancellor during the vacancy of the Holy See, 1774.]

The result of the election, which was proclaimed on February 15, 1775, was the elevation of Cardinal John Angelo Braschi to the Chair of St. Peter.

The prelate thus happily called to the first dignity in Christendom was an ecclesiastic of noble family, whom Clement XIII. had invested with the sacred purple in recognition of his admirable virtues and his erudition in civil and canon law. When the Cardinals offered the customary congratulations to the Holy Father, the Pope prophetically replied: 'Venerable Fathers, your pleasure is my misfortune.' The name chosen by the Pontiff was Pius VI.

The year 1775 is further remarkable for the death of the renowned founder of the Passionist Congregation, St. Paul of the Cross, whose long life of

eighty-one years was devoted to the spiritual regener-
ation of sinners by means of 'missions' and 'retreats'
preached in various parishes. Triumphant over serious
opposition and the calumnies of enemies, the holy
founder of the Passionists lived to see his Order
established in almost every kingdom in Europe.
Two years after his death steps were taken in Rome
to procure his beatification. More than two hundred
witnesses of rank, piety, and learning bore testimony
on oath to the heroic sanctity and miracles of the
deceased. This evidence, accompanied by petitions
from Cardinals, Bishops, heads of religious Orders,
and others, was presented to the Holy See, and in
due course laid before the Congregation of Sacred
Rites. Here Cardinal York, as Cardinal ponente,
having raised a formal objection to the introduction
of the cause, a unanimous vote of approbation was
given in its favour and the case was proceeded with.
After several years of investigation and inquiry,
Pius VI. on September 22, 1784, gave Father Paul
of the Cross the title of Venerable, this being the
first step towards that of beatification. Cardinal
York showed his thorough appreciation of the
Passionist Order by building for the Fathers at his
own expense a monastery on Mount Cavo, the highest
point of the Alban Hills. In carrying out this laud-
able work, the Cardinal unfortunately authorized an
act of vandalism which brought on the last of the
Stuarts the bitter resentment of all lovers of antiquity.
To supply the necessary building materials for the
work, the picturesque ruins of the ancient Roman
temple of Jupiter Latialis were demolished, and so
effectually that all that now remains of this once

interesting monument of paganism is a massive wall, composed of rectangular blocks of hard stone, on the south and east sides of the monastery garden. It is a subject for wonder and regret that so art-loving a Pontiff as Pius VI. did not interpose his authority to save so ancient a monument from destruction; but the rapidly increasing troubles of the Church, caused by the persecutions of the infatuated Joseph II. of Austria, left little leisure to the Pope for attending to home affairs, much less to the preservation of antiquities.

Before the close of the year 1775 the Jubilee, a period of special religious exercises and indulgences, was proclaimed in Rome. During the progress of a Jubilee, sovereigns who wish to take part in the various services and processions which mark this solemn period, have special places of honour assigned them near those allotted the Cardinals. Among the royal personages who came to Rome on this occasion for the purpose of gaining the indulgence was Ferdinand, King of Naples. The Chevalier expressed his intention of being present, but requested permission to attend as King. Cardinal York joined in this petition, and had an audience with the Holy Father on the subject; but His Holiness was not to be moved. Charles might take part in the processions as Count of Albany, but not as Charles III. The Chevalier retired to Florence, and never again attempted to press his regal claims on the authorities in Rome. At the conclusion of the Jubilee of 1775 Cardinal York, as Vice-Chancellor and Camerlengo, presided at the impressive function of walling in the Porta Sacra, which marked the final ending of a series of religious ceremonies of more than ordinary magnificence. The silver trowel with which the mason's work was formally commenced by his Eminence is now one of the historic treasures of Lord Braye.

The refusal of the Vatican to recognise him as King rankled deeply in the breast of the Chevalier, whose frame of mind was not improved by the cold reception given him about this time by the Grand Duke of Tuscany. His evil genius once more overcame him, and all his old habits returned. During the carnival season he exposed himself to the ridicule of the whole city by his continued and public state of intoxication. He went a great deal to the opera, where he lay on a couch in his box looking languidly at the performance, and drinking his favourite beverage, a sweet Cyprus wine, till quite overpowered, when his footmen carried him to his carriage and drove him home. His treatment of his consort was in perfect keeping with his general conduct. He was always either beating or abusing her, and on St. Andrew's night terrified the entire household by his attempts to strangle her. Most of his attendants quitted his service in disgust. Had it not been for the earnest entreaties of Cardinal York, the unhappy Prince would have lost his dearest friend and adviser, Mr. Caryll, of West Grinstead, Sussex, who, unable to endure the outrageous behaviour of his master, was on the point of retiring from his service. It is not surprising, in view of these events, that the Countess of Albany resolved on quitting her unfeeling husband and retiring into a convent, a project which she put into execution in November, 1780, when she temporarily entered the house of the Bianchetti, or

Dominican nuns, at Florence. From this retreat she wrote a long letter to her brother-in-law, the Cardinal, explaining the motives for the step she had taken, and asking his assistance. His Eminence replied in a very long letter, commencing as follows: 'My very dear sister, I cannot express what I have suffered in reading your letter of the ninth of this month. I have long foreseen what has happened, and the step you have taken with the sanction of the Grand Duke and Duchess guarantees the uprightness of your motives.' The Cardinal went on to say that he had consulted with the Holy Father on the subject, and had by the advice of the Pope selected a convent in Rome, to which she might retire till some arrangement could be made for her future.

The convent selected by the Cardinal was that of the Ursuline nuns, in the Via Vittoria, to which his own mother had retired during her estrangement from Prince James. Hither the Princess repaired, but, in March, 1781, she quitted this retreat for the palace of Cardinal York, at the Cancellaria, his Eminence meanwhile residing at Frascati. The Countess of Albany, who was of a strong literary turn, wished to have her library sent down from Florence, and asked the Cardinal to request the Chevalier, her husband, to forward the books. Charles, in a letter full of animosity against Louisa, replied that the books were being got ready for transmission, and enclosed a list of them 'maide by Abbé Sipolita, Language Master, and of Mathemastiques (*sic*) to ye Queen, being a very honest man, Chamellen (*sic*) to ye grande Duke.'

During the greater part of the year 1781 Cardinal

York had something far more important to attend to than the miserable domestic quarrels which were embittering his brother's last years. As Vice-Chancellor of the Apostolic See, and Camerlengo, there devolved upon him much of the government of Rome during the absence of the Pope, who had gone to Vienna to remonstrate in person with the Emperor Joseph II. for his attacks on the rights of the Church.

The Emperor, who had been left sole ruler of the Austrian dominions by the death of his mother, the pious Maria Theresa, was unhappily smitten with that love of innovation which so deeply characterized the age, and, imbued with the anti-Christian principles of the French 'philosophes,' he resolved on that oppression of the Church which has attached such an unenviable notoriety to his name.

The religious Orders, as generally happens when 'reform' is made the cloak for plunder, were the first to suffer. By imperial decree, all monastic and conventual establishments, save those engaged in teaching and works of charity, were suppressed, and their property confiscated. Other edicts, striking at the unity of the Church, followed in quick succession. No Bishop was in future to apply to Rome for consecration; no Bull, Brief, or Rescript of the Holy See was to be introduced without leave of the Government; and diocesan seminaries were replaced by two colleges, where doctrines condemned by the Church were freely taught. Finally, marriage was reduced to a civil contract, and members of the hierarchy were forbidden to accept the rank of Cardinal.

With the exception of a few courtly Bishops, the whole body of the Austrian episcopate raised its voice in protest against this shameful attempt to place the Church under the heel of the State. The Pontiff remonstrated against these proceedings through Cardinal Migazi, the *legate a latere* at Vienna. But the arts of diplomacy and entreaty were exhausted in vain; and at length Pius announced his intention of going to confer in person with the Emperor, in spite of the disapprobation of a majority of the Cardinals, who considered such a proceeding derogatory to the Papal dignity.

The result of that resolution is well known. The Pope quitted Rome on February 27, 1782, and arrived at Vienna towards the end of March. His journey was a veritable triumph, Protestants and Catholics everywhere vying with each other to show honour to the head of the Church. So great was the influx of persons into the Austrian capital to do homage to the august Pontiff, that it was feared that a famine would ensue. The visit of Pius extended over six weeks, and on leaving he was, as on his arrival, escorted a considerable part of the way by the nobility, headed by the Emperor himself. Joseph promised to do nothing prejudicial to the unity of the Church, and as an earnest of his sincerity presented the Holy Father with a gold cross set with brilliants, valued at £20,000.

The journey of the Pontiff to Vienna was far from being the fruitless undertaking that some modern historians would have us believe. The extraordinary tokens of love and loyalty manifested towards the Holy Father by millions of his spiritual children was an emphatic proof of how little a hold the infidel sophistries and corrupt example of the times had on the great mass of Catholics; while his short stay in Vienna was a distinct gain for the Church. Among the multitude of persons whom the advent of the first of Bishops attracted to the capital of the northern Cæsars was a large number of noble and wealthy Lutherans, of whom three thousand, either at the time or shortly afterwards, embraced the Catholic faith.

The Emperor Joseph lived to bitterly repent his ecclesiastical innovations, and when on his death-bed wrote to Pius with his dying hand, seeking his forgiveness and asking him to exert his authority to calm the turbulence of the Belgians, whom the Emperor's officious meddling with the venerable institutions of Church and State had driven into revolt. The Pontiff, it need scarcely be said, freely forgave his repentant son, and used his influence to compose the troubles that were threatening the remote States of the Empire.

Early in 1782 an adventurer, bearing the appropriate name of Venture, called upon Mr. Caryll, Prince Charles's steward, who happened to be in Paris, and claimed the support of Cardinal York on the ground that he was the natural son of his Eminence's father, the Old Chevalier. Mr. Caryll at once wrote to the Cardinal, informing him of the circumstances, and the latter, with that love of justice which was one of his most marked characteristics, requested Mr. Caryll to inquire into the truth of the man's story, and report to him in writing. The result of the investigation proved the utter falsehood of Venture's story. The impostor, amongst other wild statements, had asserted that he had fought in Prince Charles's army during the rebellion, although facts made it clear that he could not have been more than a child when the rising took place. To set the mind of the Cardinal completely at rest on the subject, Caryll wrote his Eminence a letter early in the spring, containing further proofs of the imposture, and concluding with these words : ' As the falsehood of his pretensions is so clearly demonstrated, I am hopeful that the fable of his origin will not give your Royal Highness a moment more of uneasiness, as it certainly will never gain credit with any who are the least informed of the character of the King.'

The visit of Gustavus III., King of Sweden, and his brother, Prince Charles, to Rome in 1783 is an event of some importance in the history of the last Stuarts. The royal visitors, who were received with every mark of distinction by the Pontifical Government, devoted much attention to the valuable museums of natural and artificial curiosities which the fine taste of Pius VI. and his immediate predecessors had constructed. But it is with the good offices of Gustavus towards Prince Charles Edward that we are mainly concerned. Shortly after his arrival in Rome the Cardinal seized on the presence of the Swedish Monarch in Rome as an excellent opportunity for making some final settlement with regard to his brother's affairs. Gustavus readily acquiesced, and sought to restore concord to the family of his host's brother. Gustavus had already met Charles Edward at Florence, and his noble and generous nature had been deeply moved by the melancholy condition of one in whose veins ran the blood of so many generations of kings. In conjunction with the Cardinal, he laboured

6

to bring about a reconciliation between the Chevalier and his consort. His efforts, however, were not attended with success, and all the kind - hearted monarch could do was to smooth the way for a legal settlement by a separation *a mensa et thoro*, which was duly agreed upon by Charles and his Countess, and ratified by the Pope on April 7, 1784. By this arrangement the Countess gave up her allowance of 15,000 crowns per annum, formerly settled on her by her husband, as well as the 4,000 allowed her by Cardinal York, who now made over this sum to his brother. The loss of these sums was compensated by a pension of £2,500 a year which her brother-in-law, the Duke de Berwick (FitzJames) procured for her from Marie Antoinette, Queen of France. On this allowance the Countess lived till the French Revolution deprived her of it. When the Revolution occurred, however, she was the wife of Vittorio Alfieri, the wealthy Florentine poet, whom she married after Prince Charles's death. She and her husband subsequently travelled in England, and were received in audience by George III. and his Queen. On their return to Florence she received a pension of £2,000 a year from the British Government, which was continued down to her death in 1824. After the death of Alfieri, in 1804, she is said to have married the French painter, Xavier Fabre, who survived her, and who, on his death, in 1837, bequeathed the fine library of the Countess, and many valuable relics of the Stuarts and Alfieri, to the museum of Montpellier, his native town. So much for the subsequent history of Louisa Countess of Albany.

In February, 1783, Charles Edward was seized with

an illness from which it was thought that he could not recover. The malady was a complication of inflammation and dropsy, and it was deemed expedient to summon his brother from Rome. Cardinal York left instantly for Florence, travelling viâ Sienna, where he stopped one night, and reaching his brother on the following day. He lodged in a monastery, near the house of the Chevalier, to whom he administered the last Sacraments of the Church. He prolonged his stay in Florence till his brother's recovery several weeks later, and then returned to Rome. In January Charles Edward had another attack of his malady, aggravated by apoplexy, and was indeed in so critical a condition that for two days he lay at the point of death. The Cardinal hastened to his bedside, but the end was not yet.

At about this time the province of Calabria, in the kingdom of Naples, was devastated by one of the most terrible series of earthquakes ever recorded. The towns of Messina, Tropea, and Reggio were reduced to ruins, the cultivation and industries of entire districts destroyed, and large portions of land near the coast violently projected into the sea. It is estimated that upwards of forty thousand persons lost their lives in this fearful calamity, while a vast number of others were plunged into the greatest suffering. To relieve their necessities extraordinary efforts were made throughout Italy. The Pope forwarded large sums of money to assist the work of relief, and by special Brief allowed the revenues of the Neapolitan monasteries to be applied for the same purpose. Cardinal York, with his accustomed generosity, set aside a considerable portion of his income for the same end, and encouraged the people of his diocese to contribute liberally towards the relief fund.

At the beginning of 1786 the Chevalier, who was now somewhat better in health, removed to Rome. He seldom appeared in public. Most of his evenings were spent in the society of the great musician, Domenico Corri, who has left us a sad picture of the last days of the unfortunate Prince. The Chevalier would sit for hours in an apartment hung with old red damask, and dimly lighted by two candles in silver sconces, while the maestro, his companion, played on the violoncello or pianoforte snatches of the music that had cheered the 'children of the mist' long long ago in the battle, the bivouac, and the march. There was not unfrequently on the table a pair of silver-mounted pistols, which the Chevalier would often take up and examine, for since the attempt on his life in 1751, by Grossart, the Whig fanatic, he had never remained unarmed. After satisfying himself that the pistols were properly primed and loaded, the Prince would replace them on the table, and then sink back again, and meditate in silence on the memories which the strains of mournful music recalled.

In the spring of 1786 he had another attack of his complaint, and recovered with difficulty. When convalescent he retired to his brother's villa at Albano, where numbers of the peasantry came to him to be touched for the King's evil. He rarely received visitors, though distinguished strangers, like Mr. Greathead, the friend of Charles James Fox, were sometimes admitted to see him. This gentleman was desirous of hearing the narrative of the Scotch rebellion from the lips of its chief actor, and on the occasion of his visit to the Chevalier studiously led the conversation up to this topic. Charles entered with zest into the subject, but the strain was too great, a fit overcame him, and he fell swooning to the floor.

Early in January, 1788, the Prince was stricken with a severe stroke of paralysis, and by the middle of the month was confined to his bed. Cardinal York, assured that his brother's life was now about to terminate, was assiduous in his attendance upon him. As the Irish Franciscan Fathers had ministered to Prince James in his last illness, the Cardinal requested the same worthy friars to attend his dying brother, and administer to him the last Sacraments of the Church. In accordance with his Eminence's wishes, Fathers James and Francis Mac-Cormick, O.S.F., took up their temporary residence at the palazzo of Charles Edward, and carefully prepared him for his rapidly approaching end.

Though the death of the Prince was now early expected, it took place, as a matter of fact, with an unexpected suddenness, and in consequence the Cardinal was not present at the closing scene of his brother's eventful career.

On January 31, 1788, the day following the anniversary of the execution of his great-grandfather, Charles I., the Chevalier had a final attack of his malady, and at half-past nine at night he expired. He had received the last Sacraments of the Chur ch and made an exemplary end.*

The Cardinal requested the Pope to allow the

* 'Tales of the Century,' by Chas. Edward and John Sobieski Stuart. London, 1846. The date of the Prince's death is given as the thirtieth, but this is a mistake.—*Author.*

deceased Prince the honours of a royal funeral. The
Holy Father, while condoling with his Eminence on
his sad loss, refused to grant his request, on the
ground that Charles had never been acknowledged
as King during his life. But the Cardinal was still
free to inter his brother as a Prince of blood royal,
and preparations for a magnificent funeral were commenced without delay. The body, after its embalmment, lay in state in the Stuart palace in Rome,
pending its removal to Frascati. Six altars were
erected in the ante-chamber of the *chapelle ardente*,
and during the thirty hours following the decease
upwards of thirty Masses of requiem were offered.
The Office for the Dead was chanted every evening in
the presence of the body by the Irish Franciscans.
When the arrangements for the obsequies were completed, the corpse was removed to the Cathedral of
Frascati, where a catafalque, surmounted by a canopy
and armorial bearings, had been prepared for its
reception. A large concourse of persons, including
many of the Italian and British nobility, filled the
church, and it was observed that everyone wore deep
mourning. So great a number of persons sought
admission to the Cathedral that it was found necessary to place troops in the square outside to prevent
the danger of overcrowding. The Cardinal, though
weighed down by grief, was the celebrant at the
requiem, assisted by several bishops and prelates.
When the absolution had been pronounced, the coffin
was borne to the crypt accompanied by the clergy,
choir, and most of the congregation, chanting the
final anthem, ' In paradisum deducant te Angeli.'
By the directions of the Cardinal, the site of the tomb

was marked by a marble slab with a Latin inscription, of which the following is the translation : 'Here lies Charles Edward, the eldest son, heir and successor of the royal dignity and paternal right of James III., King of England, Scotland, France, and Ireland, who, having taken up his abode in Rome, was styled the Count of Albany. He lived sixty-seven years and one month, and departed in peace the day before the Kalends of February in the year 1788.' The heart of the Chevalier, after being enclosed in a silver urn, was deposited in a niche in the vault, where the body of the Prince reposed till its transference shortly afterwards to St. Peter's at Rome.

As a formal assertion of his claims to the British throne, Cardinal York took two proceedings which in method and effect were in strong contrast to the warlike measures undertaken by his father and brother. The first of these was to cause himself to be silently proclaimed to the world as Henry IX. of Great Britain, France, and Ireland, by the issue of accession medals; the second to declare Prince Emanuel of Sardinia his successor to these claims. With respect to the first, he ordered a number of medals in gold and silver to be struck by his jeweller, Signor Hamerani, after the style of those issued by himself in 1774, when acting as Vice-Chancellor of the Holy See on the death of Clement XIV. Specimens of the new issue were presented to the Sovereign Pontiff, the Cardinals, and the leading personages of rank and talent in Rome. When the Duke of Sussex, George III.'s son, visited Rome some years later, his Eminence, who entertained a great esteem for him, gave him one of the impressions in gold, which the

Duke at his death in 1844 bequeathed, with his other property, to his niece, her present Majesty the Queen. These famous medals are about two inches broad, and have on the obverse the bust of Prince Henry in Cardinal's robes, while around runs the legend: ' Hen. IX. Mag. Brit. Fr. et Hib. Rex Fid. Def. Card. Ep. Frasc.' (' Henry IX., King of Great Britain, France, and Ireland, Defender of the Faith, Cardinal Bishop of Frascati '). On the reverse is represented an allegorical figure of Religion holding a Bible and cross ; at her feet is the British lion, and in the distance a view of Rome and St. Peter's. The inscription completes that of the obverse : ' Non desideriis Hominum sed voluntate Dei ' (' By the will of God, but not by the desire of men ').

With the assumption of the title of King, his Eminence did not relinquish that of Cardinal, although it had previously been the custom for members of the Sacred College to omit the title of Cardinal on succeeding to the honours of a throne. Thus, after the death of Henry III. of France in 1589, the Cardinal de Bourbon was exclusively styled Charles X., till he terminated his nominal reign of a few days' duration by voluntarily abdicating in favour of his nephew, the renowned Henri Quatre. Cardinal York, though retaining his ecclesiastical style and rank, insisted upon receiving regal honours in his household, and a sure way for a visitor, especially an Englishman, to find ready favour with his Eminence was to address him as ' Your Majesty.'

The other proceeding taken by the Cardinal with regard to his claims to the British throne was to publish a manifesto, which had been drawn up as

TABLE SHOWING THE RELATIONSHIP OF THE STUARTS WITH THE HOUSE OF SARDINIA.

Charles I. of England, = Henrietta Maria of France,
executed 1649.   d. 1669.

James II. = (2) Mary of Modena,   Henrietta Anne = Phillip, Duke of Orleans,
(1633-1701). | (1658-1718).   (1644-1670).*   brother of Louis XIV.

Charles II.,
d. 1685.

James Francis Edward, = Maria Clementina   A Prince,   Maria Louisa,   Anna Maria, m., in 1684, Victor
James III., or 'The   Sobieski   died young.   m. Charles II.   Amadeus, Duke of Savoy, and
Old Pretender'   (1702-1735).   of Spain.   afterwards King of Sardinia.
(1688-1766).

Charles Edward Louis = Louisa of Stol-   Henry Benedict   A Prince,   Charles Emanuel III.
Casimir, Charles III., or   berg-Gerden   Clement Mary   born and
The Young Pretender'   (1752-1824).   (Henry IX.),   died 1729.   Victor Amadeus III.
(1720-1788).   Cardinal Duke of   (resigned 1788).
                                              York (1725-1807).
                                                                                                 Emanuel IV. of Sardinia.

From this Prince is descended the
present Princess Maria Theresa of
Bavaria (the inheritor of the Stuart
claims), and in a less direct line
the present King of Italy, Hum-
bert.

[To face p. 89.

* The Princess Henrietta Anne, daughter of Charles I. and wife of Philip, Duke of Orleans,
was the celebrated 'Madam' of Bossuet's 'Funeral Orations.'

far back as 1764 by Signor Cataldi, the Cardinal's attorney. This document had been composed at a time when there was a likelihood that Prince Charles would die unmarried. The deed declared that in default of the Chevalier's heirs, the right to the Crown should pass, on the death of both the brothers, to Prince Emanuel, afterwards King Emanuel IV. of Sardinia, the representative of Charles I. of England, being the direct descendant of his youngest daughter, Henrietta, Duchess of Orleans. This claim is now represented by the Princess Maria Theresa, wife of the eldest son of Prince Ludwig of Bavaria. In the course of the year 1791, forty years after the bequest of the Old Chevalier to the Society of Santa Maria in Campitelli for the return of England to the Catholic faith, news arrived in Rome of the abolition of the penal laws in England after an existence of two centuries and a half. From this date the heavy cloud that had cast so deep a gloom on so many generations of adherents of the ancient faith rapidly rolled away, to make way for an epoch of ever-increasing religious liberty. These glad tidings were announced to the Holy Father by Cardinal York, to whom also fell the happy task of congratulating the students of the English College, the successors of those heroic students who, when departing for the land of persecution, had been hailed as the flowers of the martyrs by St. Philip Neri.

In the 'Life of Cardinal Consalvi,' published at Paris in 1864, there is given a full account of a nomination to the Vicariate of St. Peter's, which occasioned something like a contest between the Pope and Cardinal York. Early in 1792 Monsignor Zondari, who held the office of Vicar of the Basilica, was promoted to the Archbishopric of Sienna; whereupon the vacant vicariate reverted to Cardinal York, as the Archpriest. His Eminence, desirous of giving preferment to his friend and former protégé, Monsignor Consalvi, nominated him to the post. But before the new incumbent could take possession, it was intimated to the Cardinal that the Holy Father wished the appointment to be given to Monsignor Brancadoro, the Nuncio at Brussels, who had just then been recalled to Rome as Secretary to the Propaganda. It was also objected by the Archivist of the Chapter of St. Peter's that Consalvi, as Auditor of the Rota, was ineligible for the office, and this objection was forwarded in writing to Cardinal York. His Eminence, who discovered on investigation that the report of the Archivist was not correct, at once wrote a submissive letter to the Pontiff, pointing out this fact, and citing many cases where Vicars of the Basilica had also been Auditors of the Rota. The Pope, however, was not to be put off, and, summoning Consalvi to his presence, informed him that the vicariate must be filled up without delay, and requested him to write to this effect to Cardinal York. The Holy Father added significantly that he did not intend to insist on the election of any special candidate, as he was sure the goodwill of his Eminence would prompt him to select a candidate likely to give satisfaction to the Holy See. Consalvi wrote as desired, and the Cardinal, seeing that the wish of Pius could not be in politeness opposed any longer, replied that, using the liberty the Holy Father had granted him, he had resolved upon presenting the vacant vicariate to Monsignor Branca-

doro. Next morning Consalvi announced this decision
to the Pontiff, who remarked : ' The Cardinal Duke
has made a good choice, and we derive much satisfaction from it ; he will find that it answers the purpose
well ; tell him that from me.'

This deference to the Pontifical wishes involved a
great sacrifice to the good Cardinal, who had long
desired to bestow some substantial mark of favour on
Consalvi, in whom he had from the first discerned
evidence of that genius which was to shine forth with
such surpassing splendour a few years later. Shortly
after this occurrence, Cardinal York, in view of his
advancing years, and the natural desire he felt of
leaving his domestic and other affairs in perfect order,
resolved on drawing up his last will and testament.
In this document he appointed as executors Mon-
signors Consalvi and Cesarini, the latter being a Canon
of the Cathedral at Frascati, rector of the Seminary,
and subsequently Bishop of Milesi, *in partibus infidelium*. The will was duly drawn up by a notary,
with the exception of those clauses which related to
the aforesaid two prelates, and these the Cardinal
wrote with his own hand. To Cesarini he left the
interest on a sum of six hundred Roman scudi, or
three thousand francs, and to Consalvi six thousand
francs, payable on demand. Consalvi, whilst thanking
his Eminence for this handsome legacy, declined to
accept it, saying that he considered the fact of being
executor to his Eminence a quite sufficient token of
his esteem. The Cardinal, who was not very well
pleased with this refusal, replied that his mind was
fully made up, and Consalvi was constrained to
submit. Nine years later, when Minister of State to

Pius VII., and involved in the engrossing negotiation
of the Concordat with Napoleon, Consalvi begged His
Royal Highness to release him from the obligations of
executorship, as these duties might interfere with the
sole and undivided attention which affairs of State
demanded.   Cardinal York at once agreed, and drew
up another will, by which he gave the executorship to
Monsignor Cesarini alone.   His Eminence, however,
did not forget his old pupil in the disposal of his
property.   After the Cardinal's death, Consalvi discovered that he had been left the original sum of six
thousand francs, together with His Royal Highness's
sapphire ring, a jewel of great value.   He accepted
the ring as a precious souvenir of his old friend and
patron, but made over the money to certain old
servants of Cardinal York's.

Meanwhile, the French Revolution was rushing on
with fearful and startling rapidity.   What the fall of
the Bastille and the creation of a Constituent Assembly
had commenced, the close of the year 1792 saw
accomplished; and a republic rose on the ruins of
the ancient and splendid monarchy of France.   On
January 21, 1793, the descendant of Henri Quatre
and the Grand Monarque mounted the scaffold, and
Europe was plunged into mourning for Louis XVI.
At Rome a solemn requiem was sung for the French
King at St. Peter's, and an allocution pronounced by
Pius VI. on the truly Christian virtues and edifying
life of the royal victim to democratic fury.   Cardinal
York, in whose veins ran the royal blood of France,
by the union of his great-grandfather, Charles I., with
Henrietta Maria, daughter of King Henry IV., caused
requiems to be sung in the Cathedral at Frascati, at

which all the honours customary at the obsequies of kings were duly rendered.

During 1794, and part of 1795, the Cardinal was engaged in correspondence with the Most Honourable Charles Stuart, seventh Earl of Traquair, on the subject of certain mines in Spain to which his lordship considered he had a right. The Traquair family, though it had not openly espoused the Jacobite cause, was by sentiment and tradition entirely in sympathy with it; and one of its near relatives was William Maxwell, Earl of Nithsdale, who escaped the block, after the rising of 1715, by leaving the Tower in a disguise supplied him by his heroic wife, who remained behind in his place. The Earl of Traquair now wrote to the Cardinal to obtain his good offices as mediator in an application he had made to the Spanish Government for a concession of the exclusive right of working certain coal-mines in the peninsula. 'The Earl,' so runs the account of this negotiation, 'seems to have entertained the idea of having conferred upon him a grandeeship, and a suitable establishment in Spain, because a cadet of his family had formerly gone to that country and allied himself to one of its noble houses.' To the communication of his lordship the Cardinal replied as follows:

'In answer to your obliging letter of January 10, you may be assured that I have full cognizance of the merits and prerogatives of your family, but I cannot but remark that it is the first time in all my lifetime I have ever seen your signature or that of anyone belonging to you. That, however, has not hindered me from writing a very strong letter to the Duke of

Alcudia in your favour, and I have also taken other means to facilitate the good success of your petition. I heartily wish my endeavours may have their effect in regard of you and your son, and meanwhile be assured of my sincere esteem and kind friendship. A thousand compliments to your lady and family.

'HENRY R., Cardinal.'

'Frascati, Feb. 24, 1795.'

The Duke of Alcadia, to whom the Cardinal wrote on behalf of the Earl, was the famous Manuel de Godoy, who has obtained an unenviable notoriety in history by his intrigues with the great Napoleon, to whom he betrayed his country.

On November 7 of the same year the Cardinal again wrote as follows :

'I received with all possible satisfaction your kind letter of the 23rd Sep^bre, and am glad to find you are so much satisfied with the attentions you and your family receive from the First Minister, which persuade me your affairs will have a successful termination. For what regards the medals I got struck some years ago, I send you one of each sort ; but am now seven years older, though, God be praised, in better health than I could well expect. My most kind remembrance to Lady Traquair and your children, and, for what regards myself, you may be certain of my sincere esteem and constant kind friendship.

'HENRY R., Cardinal.

'Frascati, November 7, 1795.'

With regard to this negotiation, nothing, so far as we have been able to ascertain, ever came of it beyond the formation of a closer acquaintance between the venerable Cardinal and his remote kinsman.

The time has now arrived for narrating the story of the misfortunes which, in pursuance of the strange fatality that overhung every generation of the House of Stuart, now befell its last representative, just as he was preparing to end his days in peace.

It was not long before the revolutionists, who had already attempted to uproot the Catholic religion in France, sought a pretext for attacking the Holy See itself. One was soon found in an incident which occurred at Rome in January, 1793. A young Republican officer named Hugo Basseville, while on his way to the embassy of his country at Naples, made a short stay in Rome, and attempted to disseminate Republican ideas among the inhabitants of the Eternal City by distributing revolutionary tracts. A riot ensued, and before the police could interfere Basseville was killed. Several of the rioters were arrested, and condignly punished. But the French Directory refused to be satisfied, and declared that it held the Roman Government responsible for the officer's murder.

Pius VI., understanding that nothing short of the seizure of the patrimony of St. Peter was meditated by the French Republic, allied himself with the coalesced Powers of England, Austria, and Prussia.

In 1794 a detachment of British troops was stationed at Civita Vecchia, in the Roman States, to aid the Papal Government in checking the growth of revolution.

And here we may well pause to consider the wonderful manifestation of Providence, as shown in these events. The Roman Pontiff is no sooner abandoned by the Catholic Powers than an alliance mainly composed of Protestant States rushes to his aid. England, for over two centuries the most implacable enemy of the Apostolic See, no sooner beholds the object of its inveterate hate menaced by its foes than she sends her armies to uphold the threatened tiara, and form a serried phalanx round the Pontifical throne !*

In 1796 Napoleon Bonaparte, then rapidly rising to the front rank of the many brilliant commanders who everywhere led the armies of France to victory, invaded Italy, and by a series of the most astonishing successes, gained in the very districts where Hannibal had so repeatedly routed the legions of Rome, made himself master of the whole of the Austro-Italian territories. General Vaubois, with a powerful army, marched towards the Papal States, which were thrown into the greatest confusion at his approach. The aged Pontiff alone remained unmoved amidst the general panic, relying for aid on that Almighty power which has ever preserved the Holy See in the hour of danger. To save his people from the horrors of pillage, he consented to the enormous exactions of the French General, and agreed to hand over the sum of 20,000,000 francs, a large quantity of horses and

---

* In the South Kensington Museum there is a fine painting representing several British officers in the act of being presented to Pius VI. Their names were: Major, afterwards General Brown Clayton, Captain Head, and Lieutenant the Hon. Pierce Butler. The Holy Father is depicted placing a plumed dragoon helmet on the head of Major Brown Clayton, and at the same time offering up a prayer for the King of England and the welfare of the noble British nation.

provisions, and a number of the finest paintings and statues the galleries of Rome possessed. Before these conditions could be fulfilled, the French were forced to retire before a relieving army of Austrians ; but the check was only momentary. After the victories of the Republican armies at Senico and Ancona, the Pope found himself required to pay an additional sum of 30,000,000 francs as a penalty for the encouragement he was supposed to have given the Austrians. The resources of the Pontifical treasury were strained to the utmost to meet these monstrous demands, and the nobility and wealthy classes of Rome disposed of their private jewels that they might contribute to the amount demanded. Cardinal York, as his share in the good work, parted with a magnificent ruby, the size of a pigeon's egg, valued at £60,000, once the property of John Sobieski. These concessions delayed, but could not avert, the fatal day. On December 28, 1797, a handful of revolutionists, headed by General Duphot, sought to revive the insane attempt of Basseville, and plant ' the banner of freedom on the Capitol.' A collision with the troops ensued, and Duphot and several of his associates were shot. The Directory, glad of this opportunity for finally annexing the States of the Church, gave orders to General Berthier to march on Rome with an army of 18,000 men.

No resistance was made to the advancing host, and on February 10, 1798, the French troops poured into the Eternal City. The cannon of the invaders thundered along the deserted streets, the tree of liberty was planted on the Campo Vecino, and the ' Roman Republic, the sister and ally of France,' was proclaimed from the Capitol, amidst the roar

7

of artillery, the strains of the Marseillaise, and the invocation of the names of Brutus and Cato. Meanwhile the halls of the Vatican resounded with the shouts of an exultant soldiery eager in the work of pillage. The apartments were stripped to the bare walls, and the Vicar of Christ stood alone amidst flashing sabres and bristling bayonets. The very ring was torn from his finger, while, in tones of angry menace, the renunciation of temporal power was demanded from him. For response, the old man fearlessly replied that, though they hewed him in pieces, never would he surrender one jot or tittle of the Church's patrimony, of which he was not the master, but the guardian. He was led away to die in captivity at Valence; the tricolour waved over the Castle of St. Angelo, and an exulting world triumphantly declared that the Papacy was no more.

At the time the French troops pillaged Rome, the ' Cardinal was living quietly at his villa near Frascati, his life being spent in the discharge of his episcopal duties, and in the exercise of charity. The entrance of the invaders was the signal for a number of disaffected persons to rise in revolt, in the hope of the plunder. The villas of the Cardinals, nobility, and wealthy classes, which studded the fair expanse of the Campagna were marked out as the objects of immediate attention, and among these, of course, that of Cardinal York. His Eminence, who apprehended an attack from the revolutionary banditti, took steps to save at least some portion of his property from seizure by hiding as much of it as he could so dispose of among the cottages of the neighbouring peasantry, whose affection for the good Cardinal was unbounded.

On February 9 news was hastily brought that a large mob of revolutionists was in the neighbourhood. The aged Cardinal was compelled to forsake the Villa Muti at once, and leave his beautiful house, with its wealth of historic and artistic treasures, to the mercy of the pillagers. Fortunately for him, and all those who were flying from the revolutionists, General Mack, the Austrian commander, held the district between Albano and Naples, to which city the Cardinal now directed his journey. There he might have rested—at least, for a time—had not the disgraceful behaviour of Mack's soldiers at Terni opened the road to Naples to the French, with the result that the Court of Naples was forced to betake itself to flight. On the night of December 21 the King and Queen, with the royal family and ministers, embarked on board the British fleet for Sicily. Cardinal York, at the special invitation of their Majesties, accompanied them, and in due course the fugitives arrived at Messina.

It was now the intention of his Eminence to make for Corfu, a locality sufficiently remote from the revolutionary troubles, and thence to proceed to Venice. He was, however, prevented from starting immediately by contrary winds, but after considerable delay was enabled to set sail in a Greek merchant-vessel. On his arrival at Corfu he delayed starting for Venice till he should receive further intelligence concerning the progress of the Republican cause in Italy. On being informed that no change for the better had taken place in the political outlook, he sailed for Venice, which he reached early in May. On landing in this city, the Cardinal took up his residence in a humble lodging near the Rialto, where he maintained himself for a time by the sale of some silver plate which he had brought with him. His scanty means were soon exhausted, and at length this aged Prince, the last of a race of Kings, Vice-Chancellor of the Holy See, and Cardinal of the Holy Roman Church, was forced to seek the assistance of a neighbouring monastery to prevent himself from perishing from sheer want !

The *Times* newspaper, in a leading article, in its issue for February 28, 1800, two years later, thus commented on the series of events that had reduced this representative of British royalty to such distress :

' The Cardinal of York, the brother of Charles Edward, early dedicated himself to a life congenial with the habits of his mind. Placid, humane, and temperate, he sought consolation for the misfortunes of his ancestors in a scrupulous observance of the duties of his religion, apparently secured in his retirement from the storms and vicissitudes but too often attendant upon political life. The malign influence of the star which had so strongly marked the fate of so many of his illustrious ancestors was not exhausted ; and it was peculiarly reserved for the Cardinal of York to be exposed to the shafts of adversity at a period of life when least able to struggle with misfortune. At the advanced age of seventy-five he is driven from his episcopal residence, his house is sacked, his property confiscated, and constrained to seek his personal safety in flight upon the seas under every aggravated circumstance that could affect his health or fortune.'

What, indeed, would have been the ultimate fate

of the last male descendant of Robert Bruce, had
not an intercessor been happily found to represent
his case in the most effective manner to the British
Government, we cannot say. This timely spokesman
was the famous Cardinal Stephen Borgia, who, like
Cardinal York, was living in exile at Venice. A
member of the historic family of Borgia, his Eminence
was born at Velletri in 1731, and at the age of nineteen
had established his reputation for learning sufficiently
to be elected a member of the Etruscan Academy of
Cortona, one of the many societies devoted to the
study of antiquities and elegant literature which were
then to be found in every town and city of Italy. Of
easy fortune and abundant leisure, he had ample
opportunity for collecting a fine museum of antique
bronzes, cameos, coins, and medals, which soon
acquired a European reputation. In 1770 Pope
Clement XIV. made him Secretary to the Propaganda,
a post which enabled him to acquire a valuable stock
of Oriental idols, curiosities, and manuscripts. His
splendid talents as an antiquarian scholar were at
length fitly rewarded in 1789, when Pius VI. bestowed
upon him the red hat as Cardinal Priest. When the
Revolution drove him from Rome he betook himself,
with the majority of the other fugitives, to Venice,
where he discovered his old friend Cardinal York in
the forlorn condition we have described.

Among the numerous Englishmen who claimed the
happy privilege of friendship with Cardinal Borgia
was Sir John Coxe-Hippisley, M.P., who played an
important part in the politics of the day, as an
advocate of Catholic emancipation. To Sir John,
therefore, Cardinal Borgia now addressed himself in

the following letter, which gives a full account of the many losses and calamities undergone by Cardinal York.

'It is greatly affecting to me to see so great a personage, the last descendant of his royal house, reduced to such distressed circumstances, having been barbarously stripped by the French of all his property; and if they deprived him not of his life also, it was through the mercy of the Almighty, who protected him in his flight both by sea and land; the miseries of which, nevertheless, greatly injured his health at the advanced age of seventy-five, and produced a very grievous sore in one of his legs. Those who are well informed of this most worthy Cardinal's domestic affairs have assured me that since his flight, having left behind him his rich and magnificent movables, which were all sacked and plundered both at Rome and Frascati, he has been supported by the silver plate he had taken with him, and which he began to dispose of at Messina, and I understand that in order to supply his wants a few months ago in Venice he has sold all that remained. Of the jewels he possessed very few remain, as the most valuable had been sacrificed in the well-known contributions to the French, our destructive plunderers; and with respect to his income, after having suffered the loss of 48,000 Roman crowns annually, by the French Revolution, the remainder was lost also by the fall of Rome, namely, the yearly sum of 10,000 crowns assigned him by the Apostolic Chamber, and also his particular funds in the Roman banks. The only income he has left is that of his benefices in Spain, which amounts to

14,000 crowns, but which, as it is only payable at present in paper, is greatly reduced by the disadvantage of exchange, and even that has remained unpaid for more than a year, owing, perhaps, to the interrupted communication with that kingdom. But here it is necessary that I should add that the Cardinal is heavily burdened with the annual sum of 4,000 crowns for the dowry of the Countess of Albany, his sister-in-law; 3,000 to the mother of his deceased niece; and 15,000 for divers annuities of his father and brother. Nor has he credit to supply the means of acquitting these obligations. This picture, nevertheless, which I present to your friendship may well excite the compassion of everyone who will reflect on the high birth, the elevated dignity, and the advanced age, of the personage whose situation I now sketch in the plain language of truth, without resorting to the aid of eloquence! I will only entreat you to communicate it to those distinguished persons who have influence in your Government, persuaded as I am that the English magnanimity will not suffer an illustrious personage of the same nation to perish in misery! But here I pause, not wishing to offend your national delicacy, which delights to act from its own generous dispositions rather than from the impulse and urgency of others.'

On the receipt of Cardinal Borgia's letter, Sir John conveyed it to his friend, Mr. Andrew Stewart, a near relative of Mr. Archibald Stewart, and well known in his day for his letters on the famous Douglas peerage case, which took up the attention of the law lords from 1771 to 1790. Mr. Stewart, who entered warmly into the affair, drew up a memorial on the subject, which Mr. Dundas, afterwards Lord Melville, presented to the King.   His Majesty George III., whose friendly dispositions towards his unfortunate relatives the Stuarts had long been so well and widely known, was deeply affected at the melancholy account of the destitution into which the venerable Cardinal of York had fallen, and at once expressed his intention of making a suitable allowance to his Eminence as long as he should be pleased to avail himself of it. This assistance, it may be added, was at first only intended to be paid until the straitened circumstances of the Cardinal should improve, though in the sequel the royal pension was continued to the time of His Royal Highness's death.

Such, then, being the resolution of the King, His Majesty immediately desired Lord Minto, the English Ambassador at Vienna, to request the Cardinal in as delicate terms as possible to accept an annual sum of £5,000 as a proof of his Sovereign's affection and esteem.   This Lord Minto was the Gilbert Elliot familiar to all readers of Sir Walter Scott's poems, whose services as a diplomatist were rewarded with an earldom shortly before his death in 1814.

Upon receipt of the King's commands, Lord Minto despatched one of his attachés, Mr. Charles Oakeley, son of Sir Charles Oakeley, Bart., to convey the royal will and pleasure to Cardinal York, whose sentiments on this occasion are described in the following letter written by him to the English Ambassador:

'With the arrival of Mr. Oakeley, who has been this morning with me, I have received by his discourses, and much more by your letter, so many tokens of your regard, singular considerations, and attention for my person, as obliges me to abandon all ceremony, and to begin abruptly to assure you, my dear Lord, that your letters have been most acceptable to me in all shapes and regards. I did not in the least doubt of the noble way of thinking of your beneficent sovereign ; but I did not expect to see in writing so many and so obliging expressions, and well calculated for the persons who receive them and understand their force, to impress in their minds a most lively sense of tenderness and gratitude, which I own to you oblige me more than the generosity spontaneously imparted. . . . I am much obliged to you to have indicated to me the way I may write unto Coutts, the Court bankers, and shall follow your friendly insinuations. In the meantime I am very desirous that you should be convinced of my sentiments of sincere esteem and friendship, with which, my dear Lord, with all my heart I embrace you.

' HENRY, Cardinal.'

His Eminence did not neglect to send his sincerest thanks to Sir John Coxe-Hippisley for his kind and opportune representation of his case to the English Court. A few weeks before the conclusion of the Conclave which elected Pius VII. to the Papal throne, vacated by the death of Pius VI., he addressed the following letter to him :

' VENICE, *February* 26, 1800.

' Your letters fully convince me of the cordial interest you take in all that regards my person, and

I am happy to acknowledge that principally I owe to your friendly efforts and to those of your friends the succour generously granted to relieve the extreme necessities into which I have been driven by the present dismal circumstances. I cannot sufficiently express how sensible I am to your good heart, and write these few lines in the first place to contest to you these my most sincere and grateful sentiments, and then to inform you that by means of Mr. Oakeley, an English gentleman who arrived here last week, I have received a letter from Lord Minto from Vienna, advising me that he had orders from his Court to remit to me at present the sum of £2,000, and that in the month of July next I may again draw, if I desire it, for another equal sum. The letter is written in so extremely genteel and obliging a manner, and with expressions of singular regard and consideration for me, that I assure you excited in me most particular and lively sentiments, not only of satisfaction for the delicacy with which the affair has been managed, but also of gratitude for the generosity which has provided for my necessity. I have answered Lord Minto's letter, and gave it on Saturday last to Mr. Oakeley, who was to send it by that evening's post to Vienna, and have written in a manner that I hope will be to his Lordship's satisfaction. I own to you that the succours granted could not be more timely, for without it it would have been impossible for me to subsist, on account of the absolutely irreparable loss of all my income; the very funds being also destroyed, so that I would otherwise have been reduced for the short remainder of my life to languish in misery and indigence. I would not lose a moment's time to apprize you of all this, and am very certain that your experimented good heart will find proper means to make known in an energetical and proper manner these sentiments of my grateful acknowledgments. The signal obligations I am under to Mr. Andrew Stuart for all that he has with so much cordiality on this occasion done to assist me, renders it for me indispensable to desire that you may return him my most sincere thanks, assuring him that his health and welfare interest me extremely; and that I have with great pleasure received from General Heton [query, Seton] the genealogical history of our family, which he was so kind as to send me, and hope that he will from the General have already received my thanks for so valuable a proof of his attention to me. In the last place, if you think proper, and occasion should offer itself, I beg you to make known to the other gentlemen who also have co-operated my most grateful acknowledgments, with which, my dear Sir John, with all my heart I embrace you.

'Your best of friends,
'HENRY, Cardinal.'

'To SIR J. C. HIPPISLEY, Bart.,
'London.'

In the following May, just after the Conclave, the Cardinal again writes :

'VENICE, *May*, 1800.

'DEAR SIR JOHN,
'I have not words to explain the deep impression your obliging favour of March 31 made on me, your and Mr. Andrew Stuart's most friendly and warm exertions in my behalf, the humane and

benevolent conduct of your Ministers, your gracious Sovereign's noble and spontaneous generosity, the continuance of which, you certify me, depends on my need of it, were all ideas which crowded together on my mind, and filled me with the most lively senti-ments of tenderness and heart-felt gratitude. What return can I make for so many and so signal proofs of disinterested benevolence? Dear Sir John, I confess I am at a loss how to express my feelings. I am sure, however, and very happy that your good heart will make you fully conceive the sentiments of mine, and induce you to make known in an adequate and con-venient manner, to all such as you shall think proper, for me my most sincere acknowledgments.

'With pleasure I have presented your compliments to the Cardinals and other personages you mention, who all return you their sincere thanks; the Canon, in particular, now Monsignore, being a domestic prelate of His Holiness, begs you to be persuaded of his constant respect and attachment to you.

'My wishes would be completely satisfied, should I have the pleasure, as I most earnestly desire, to see you again at Frascati, and be able to assure you by word of mouth of my most sincere esteem and affec-tionate gratitude.

'Your best of friends,
'HENRY, Cardinal.'

'SIR JOHN COXE-HIPPISLEY,
    'Grosvenor Street, London.'

The bestowal of the pension on the Cardinal by King George III. caused the greatest satisfaction among all classes, and at the annual banquet of the Literary Fund for the year 1800 the following lines

in praise of the royal beneficence were recited by
Mr. Fitzgerald :

'Illustrious Isle! Fair Freedom's last retreat!
The throne of honour! pure Religion's seat!
Object of Europe's envy and her hate,
Still shalt thou stand amidst the nations great;
Still shall the persecuted stranger find
Thy happy shores the refuge of mankind,
And the last Prince of Darnley's house shall own
His debt of gratitude to Brunswick's throne!'

It must be stated, indeed, that the Cardinal had a
very just claim for assistance on the Government of
this country. A large part of the sum voted by
Parliament for his grandmother, Queen Mary, consort
of James II., had never been paid, although several
efforts had been made by the Cardinal's family,
through the Court of France, to recover it. The
pension now granted his Eminence had, however, no
reference to this outstanding claim, but was made
purely from the liberality and goodwill of the King
of England towards an unfortunate member of his
own family.*

With regard to the Conclave to which we have
referred, a few words will suffice. On August 29,
1799, the aged Pius VI. expired at Valence, worn out
by the sufferings of mind and body he had lately
undergone. The enemies of the Papacy exulted over
the supposed annihilation of the Holy See, but the
Cardinals assembled at Venice and calmly proceeded
to elect another Pontiff.

About thirty-five members of the Sacred College
were able to comply with the invitations of the Cardinal Dean, John Francis Albani, to repair to the

---

* One account, however, says that out of delicacy to the
Cardinal the pension of King George III. was paid him as if in
discharge of this debt.

Church of San Georgio at Venice, where the Conclave was to assemble under the protection of the allied Powers. Cardinal York acted as Sub-Dean during the proceedings of the election, while Cardinal Consalvi, as Auditor of the Rota, was selected as Secretary.

At the outset of the election the voting went very much in favour of Cardinal Bellisoni, Bishop of Cesena, and formerly Nuncio at Lisbon, a prelate much esteemed for his amiability and many virtues, but towards the conclusion the votes were transferred to Cardinal Gregorio Chiaramonti, who, after the final scrutiny, taken on March 13, 1800, was declared elected to the throne of St. Peter, and on the following day was proclaimed to the astonished world as Pius VII.

The new Pope, thus unexpectedly raised up by Providence to rule the Church amidst many tribulations, was a Benedictine monk, who had been honoured with the cardinalitial purple by Pius VI. One of the first acts of the Holy Father, after the Conclave, was to raise Consalvi from the rank of Cardinal Deacon to that of Cardinal Priest, with the title of Santa Maria ad Martyres, an event which gave great satisfaction to that distinguished prelate's old friend Cardinal York, whose desire to see his undoubted genius receive the recognition it deserved has already been commented upon in these pages.

We must now pass on quickly to the account of Cardinal York's return to his beloved diocese. On July 3, 1800, the Pope re-entered Rome in triumph, and the Holy City quickly assumed its normal aspect. One of the first to follow Pius VII. was Cardinal York, who made the homeward journey by easy stages, and reached his episcopal residence a few weeks after the

Pontifical occupation of the Vatican. The greatest enthusiasm prevailed in and about Frascati. His Eminence's carriage was drawn into the town by the inhabitants, who at night illuminated the entire place in honour of their beloved Bishop's safe return. Most of his splendid effects had been lost beyond recall. But such as could be recovered were quickly back again in the Cardinal's palace, which the restoration of his benefice and the King of England's pension enabled him to once more furnish and appoint in a style worthy of a Prince of royal and ecclesiastical rank.

Rome being restored to order and tranquillity, we may proceed to contemplate the last of the Stuarts as he was in the seclusion of private life, surrounded by his household and the many friends who came to visit him at Frascati.

Valentine, Lord Cloncurry, in his ' Life and Times,' published in 1849, has left us some highly interesting details of Cardinal York in these his closing days. His lordship, who had become involved in the Irish troubles of 1798, was advised by his friends to spend a few years on the Continent till such time as his indiscretion had become forgotten by the Government. He passed a good deal of his time in Italy, and while in Rome was a frequent guest at the table of Cardinal York, who liked to have about him young men of talent and originality, such as Lord Cloncurry undoubtedly was. It is from the accounts which he has given of these visits that the following details are mostly drawn.

With regard to money matters, the Cardinal, in spite of his heavy losses during the period of the Revolution, was extremely well off. In addition to the emoluments from his offices and benefices, he had the income provided by George III., which alone in Italy was equal to £20,000 a year at least. His Eminence, when at Frascati, often amused himself and his friends by little dramatic entertainments, performed in his drawing-room by some of the students of the college attached to his seminary. A favourite piece with the Cardinal was the scene representing Sancho Panza and his physician during the reign of the Squire in the island of Barataria.

His Royal Highness, being now an invalid, was placed under strict regimen by his medical advisers, but this did not prevent him from occasionally striving playfully with the attendants, as he sat at table, for certain savoury dishes of which he was fond, but which the physicians absolutely forbade him to touch.

During one of his visits to Frascati Lord Cloncurry gave the Cardinal a telescope, to which the latter had taken a fancy, and received in return one of the large medals struck by his Eminence in honour of his 'unsubstantial throne.' The value of the telescope was greatly enhanced in the eyes of the Cardinal by the fact that it was of English manufacture, goods made in this country being then highly prized on the Continent for their finish and excellence. As an instance of this appreciation of English manufactures it is recorded that an ordinary English dressing-case given by Lord Cloncurry's sister to the Princess Messina was the envy and admiration of all the ladies of Rome, to whom it was occasionally shown as a great favour.

Mr. Forsyth, the celebrated Scotch traveller, in his work entitled ' Italy,' says that on being presented to his Eminence on one occasion, during the summer of 1802, his introducer, an Irish gentleman living in Rome, either pronounced his name badly, or else the Cardinal did not catch it aright, for his Eminence remarked facetiously that although he had heard of 'second sight' in Scotland, he had never heard of 'Foresight' in England; whereupon the few by-standers who knew English laughed heartily. Learning from Mr. Forsyth that his grandfather had fallen on behalf of the Stuarts, the Cardinal at once took great interest in him, drove him in his carriage to Frascati, and invited him to dinner, where he placed him on his right hand. The other guests present at table were a Bishop, a Sardinian Duke, and several of the lesser Roman nobility. His Eminence sat with an interval for one person on each side—an honour due to his dual rank. The Cardinal used the plainest table-ware, although the rest of the company were served on gold and silver plate. Even his coffee-cup was of inferior material to the cups used by his guests. He showed Mr. Forsyth a dog, adding significantly that it was a 'King Charles.' The dog in question attached itself to his Eminence one day as he was leaving St. Peter's, and as it was of the breed just named, the Cardinal often referred to it as a proof of his royal blood, since dogs of this species are fabled to detect instinctively members of the House of Stuart. The costume of His Royal Highness on this occasion is described by Mr. Forsyth as being alternately of red and black, viz., red skull-cap, black coat lined with red silk, black knee-breeches, and red silk stockings. In features, says the same informant, he was ruddy and handsome.

8

To the very last Cardinal York insisted on being paid sovereign honours, and Lord Cloncurry never omitted to address him as 'Your Majesty,' thus going a step farther than the Duke of Sussex, who always styled him 'Your Royal Highness.' Augustus Frederick, Duke of Sussex, as most of our readers are aware, was the sixth and most estimable of all the sons of George III. After completing his studies at the University of Göttingen, he resided for some years in Rome, where he was warmly received by the reigning Pontiff, Pius VI., who caused every honour and attention to be shown him. It was while in Rome that he married the Lady Augusta Murray, daughter of the Earl of Dunmore, a marriage which was rendered null and void by the tyrannous Royal Marriage Act of 1772. From the first the Duke had encountered serious obstacles to his projected union. The Catholic Church, while tolerating marriages between Catholics and Protestants, does not allow her clergy to perform the ceremony between two Protestants; and although the Duke applied to all the priests in Rome, and had several interviews with his friend Cardinal York on the subject, he could, of course, obtain no suspension of this important law. After much delay he was married in the palace where he was staying by the Rev. Mr. Gunn, an Anglican clergyman, who happened to be in Rome on business.

The Duke of Sussex was not the only member of the House of Hanover who sought the friendship of the last of the race which that House had supplanted on the British throne. Like all the princes of his family, Cardinal York claimed to possess the power of touching for the King's Evil, and, on the death of his brother, caused a number of touch pieces to be made for the purpose. These were small medals of gold, having on the obverse the figure of St. Michael trampling Satan under foot, with the legend, 'Soli Deo Gloria.' On the reverse was stamped a ship of war in full sail, and the inscription in Latin : ' The most Reverend Henry IX., by the Grace of God King of Great Britain, France, Ireland, and Wales, Bishop of Frascati.' It is said on good authority that one of the brothers of George III. took a journey to Frascati to receive in orthodox fashion from the hand of Henry IX. the healing touch which had been denied to the rulers of his own dynasty. The Master of Ceremonies to the Cardinal did not, according to this statement, know how to settle the question of reception and introduction ; but finally it was arranged so that the two princes should meet one another while out driving. The plan succeeded admirably, for, the carriages having met, the Cardinal was attracted by the royal arms of England on the panels of the stranger's coach, and on being informed that the brother of ' the Elector of Hanover ' was within, at once invited him to his villa, where the Prince underwent the ceremony of receiving the royal touch, though with what result history sayeth not.

When the Cardinal went to Frascati for the first time after his accession to the empty title of King, a great number of peasants brought their children or relatives to be cured of the scrofula (the veritable King's Evil), and it is said that the gold pieces with which the rite was performed are treasured as precious relics in the families of many of their descendants to this day.

Of the popularity of Cardinal York among all classes of persons we have already spoken. The late Cardinal Wiseman, in his ' Recollections of the Last Four Popes,' says that when he first went to Frascati, which was shortly after his arrival in Rome as a student of the English College, in 1818, the place was full of kindly reminiscences of the last of the Stuarts, 'all demonstrative of his singular goodness and simplicity of character.' This is well illustrated by the following story told of His Royal Highness by the same informant :

' When he first came to Rome, so ignorant was he of the value of coins that once, having been shown some place or object of curiosity, he was asked what should be given to the attendant. As he was puzzled, his chamberlain suggested: " Shall I give him a zecchino ?"—a gold piece worth about ten shillings. Thinking that the diminutive termination must indicate small coin, the Duke replied : " I think that is too little ; give him a grosso "—a silver fivepence.'

It must be remarked that in the early part of his life the Cardinal of York left the management of his monetary and other temporal affairs to his Vicar-General and Grand Chamberlain ; but even allowing this, it is scarcely possible that he could have been so indifferent to mundane matters as to be ignorant of the value of current coin, so the story may be looked upon either as apocryphal or, at least, very much exaggerated. What has been said of the Cardinal's kindness, liberality, and genial disposition, certainly ill accords with those accounts which have described his Eminence as ' a dull, bigoted man,' or which represent Pius VI. as declaring, after an interview with the

Cardinal, that he did not wonder the English had been glad to get rid of so tiresome a race as the Stuarts.

The complete difference wrought in his fortune and family affairs by the great political and social change that had come over Europe since 1792 made it necessary for his Eminence to make a fresh disposal of his property, especially as his executor, Monsignor Cesarini, was in indifferent health, and his other executor, Cardinal Consalvi, had been released from his obligation. Cardinal York therefore caused a second will to be drawn up on July 15, 1802. It commences thus :

' We, Henry Benedict Mary, son of James III., King of England, Scotland, France, and Ireland, Cardinal of the Holy Roman Church, Bishop of Frascati, considering that we are mortal, and not knowing the time and the hour when Almighty God will be pleased to call us to Him, have resolved, now that we are in good health and in the full enjoyment of our faculties, to make our last disposition, and to provide as well as to that which relates to our funeral, as for the salvation of our soul and our temporal affairs.'

The will, which is of considerable length, declared Monsignor Cesarini, Bishop of Milesi, ' our universal proprietary heir, with full liberty to enjoy and to dispose of our inheritances, moveable and real goods, rights as above named, without any condition or restriction whatever.' The will concludes :

'Finally, it is our intention to renew here and to consider as expressly inserted in it our protest deposited in the Acts of the notary Cataldi, on the

27th of January, 1764, and published on the 30th of
January, 1788, at the death of our most serene brother,
relative to the transmission of our rights of succession
to the throne and crown of England in behalf of the
Prince, on whom they devolve by right (*de jure*), by
proximity of blood, and by right of succession.   We
declare to remit these rights to him in the most
explicit and solemn form.   Such is our last will and
testamentary disposition, dictated word by word (*de
verbo ad verbum*).   It is our will that it have
perpetual validity, and the best and most valid title
competent to us (to give it).

' Given at our residence in Frascati, on the fifteenth
day of July, 1802.

' HENRY ROI.'

The last extract quoted from the Cardinal's will
refers to the King of Sardinia, whose relationship with
the Stuarts has been already mentioned.   Monsignor
Cesarini did not long survive his Eminence, dying at
Rome early in 1808, when his place as executor was
taken by a Mr. Tassoni, a gentleman in whom he had
the utmost confidence.   Mr. Tassoni also received the
entire quantity of State papers and private documents
belonging to the Stuarts, amounting to over half a
million in number.   A certain Dr. Robert Watson,
who, it is said, had been secretary to Lord George
Gordon during the riots of 1780, entered into negotiations with Tassoni for the purchase of these, and the
bargain was already concluded when the Papal
Government intervened, on the ground that the papers
in question were too valuable for any subject to possess.
In 1817 Cardinal Consalvi, the Minister of State,

presented them to the Prince Regent, afterwards George IV., by whom they were in great part placed in the royal library at Windsor.

In the September of 1803 Cardinal Albani, whose abilities and attainments have been already noted, and who since 1775 had filled the offices of Bishop of Ostia and Dean of the Sacred College, died at his episcopal residence, in the eighty-fourth year of his age. By the decease of this illustrious Prince of the Church, the deanship of the Cardinals and the See of Ostia and Velletri devolved on the Duke of York, who was in consequence formally translated to the superior See on November 20. His Eminence, who had been now Bishop of Frascati for over forty years, was much grieved at the prospect of having to quit a town which had become so dear to him by reason of long associations and the attachment of its inhabitants to his person. He communicated his regret to the Holy Father, and Pius VII., pleased at being able to show a proof of his regard for the venerable Cardinal, at once granted him a special privilege by which he might retain the episcopal palace of Frascati, although no longer Bishop of the town.

During the last four years of his life Cardinal York spent nearly the whole of his time at Frascati, rarely going to Rome, except when business of especial necessity called him. His house, as has been before mentioned, was ever open to such of his countrymen as cared to avail themselves of his hospitality, while his ample fortune was largely employed in succouring those whom misfortune or folly had reduced to extremity.

Throughout the two years immediately preceding

his death the Cardinal suffered very much from the mild form of epilepsy known as *petit mal*, which caused him long lapses of memory, and almost debarred him from performing even the least arduous of his episcopal duties. The administration of the diocese during this time was attended to by his coadjutor and Vicar-General.

To the very last his Eminence continued to take the liveliest interest in the seminary at Frascati, of which institution he might in truth be called the second founder, and although it was no longer under his jurisdiction, the Cardinal made over to it considerable sums of money as endowments in perpetuity.

About a year after his translation to the See of Ostia, his Eminence lost his old and devoted friend, Cardinal Stephen Borgia, whose letter to Sir John Coxe-Hippisley had been instrumental in drawing the attention of the Court of St. James's to the misfortunes of His Royal Highness. This excellent Cardinal died at Lyons on November 23, 1804, while accompanying the Pope to Paris for the coronation of Napoleon as Emperor of the French.

The narrative of events has brought us now to the closing scene in the life of Prince Henry Stuart.

Cardinal York was seized with his mortal sickness towards the end of June, 1807. The fever—for such was the complaint—gradually gained upon his aged and enfeebled frame, so that, before the end of the month his physicians assured him that his death was near. From the first day of his illness his Eminence caused an altar to be erected in his apartment, at which his chaplain, Monsignor Cesarini, said Mass every morning. The Pope, Pius VII., expressed the utmost concern for the critical condition of the venerable Cardinal, and had himself informed by frequent couriers of the progress of the disease. As days passed by and the final dissolution was hourly expected, the road between Rome and Frascati became covered with carriages of prelates, princes, and others, who came to make inquiries at the palace gates concerning the condition of the dying Cardinal. On the morning of July 13 the last agony commenced, and the entire household was summoned to his Eminence's bedside. The Recommendation of a Departing Soul and the other prayers proper for this solemn occasion, were recited alternately by Cardinal Doria, who had succeeded the Duke in the See of Frascati, and Monsignor Cesarini. These devotions were continued till the Duke breathed his last, early in the afternoon.

The death of the Cardinal Duke of York occurred on the anniversary of his translation to the See of Frascati, when he had been a member of the Sacred College sixty years and ten days. As he was at the time of his decease Vice-Chancellor of the Apostolic See, the Holy Father gave orders that the lying in state of the Cardinal should take place in the palace of the Cancellaria, under the shadow of the mighty dome beneath which the last princes of the ancient Stuart line have found a final resting-place. In pursuance of the Pontifical order, the body of the deceased was taken to Rome on the evening of July 16. A large number of coaches swelled the funeral cortège, and the hearse was accompanied by a troop of cavalry. In the great reception-hall of the Cancellaria a bed of state was prepared, and the whole apartment was transformed into a suitable mortuary chamber by means of velvet hangings, hatchments and candelabra. The body of the dead Cardinal was vested in the full robes pertaining to his exalted rank as Prince of the Church, and at the feet were placed the mitre and crozier, together with the Cardinal's hat, and a coat-of-arms emblazoned with the armorial bearings of England. A company of the Swiss Guard kept watch and ward round the catafalque, and the stream of spectators who came to gaze upon all that was mortal of the titular Henry IX. passed behind a strong wooden barrier draped with black velvet. The lying in state terminated on the evening of the nineteenth.

The last solemn rites accorded the Cardinal were in every way worthy of one whose death brought to a close a dynasty that had filled a throne for upwards of four centuries. So dense was the crowd that thronged St. Peter's that one might have thought all Rome had gathered together to assist at the last sad offices.

Cardinal Doria, who now succeeded His Royal Highness as Dean of the Sacred College, pontificated, in the presence of the Sovereign Pontiff, more than thirty Cardinals, and a large number of Bishops and lesser prelates. The foreign ambassadors in Rome occupied their accustomed places, and the number of titled and distinguished personages was unusually great. On the same day another solemn Mass of requiem for the repose of the Cardinal's soul was sung in the cathedral at Frascati, which was filled to the very doors. The celebrant was the dean, and the funeral oration was pronounced by Father Marco Mastrofini, Professor of Philosophy at the seminary.

When the last sad rites had been brought to a close

at St. Peter's, the coffin was removed to the crypt and interred with the other members of the Stuart family in that hallowed spot which to the remotest times must make every Englishman who visits the mighty Basilica pause and reflect on the ashes it contains. The body of Charles Edward had already been removed from its temporary resting-place at Frascati, and in close proximity to the mouldering dust of James III. and Charles III. the body of Henry IX. was now laid. Masses continued to be said for the deceased, both at Rome and Frascati, for many days after the interment, but no monument marked for many years to come the place where rested in peace the mortal remains of the three Kings of England by the Grace of God but not by the will of man.

With the exception of benefactions to his servants, and some donations to various charities, the bulk of Cardinal York's large fortune went to found bursaries for the education of students of the Scots College in Rome, of which institution he is considered one of the foremost benefactors.*

One more remark on the subject of the Cardinal's testamentary dispositions may not be without interest. When James II. fled from England in 1688 he carried with him, amongst other hastily-collected treasures, the crown and coronation-ring — insignia destined never again to be worn by his descendants. As some sort of acknowledgment of the bounty shown him by the House of Hanover, the Cardinal on his death-bed

---

* Among the bequests of the Cardinal to the Scots College was the original copy of the proclamation which Charles Edward caused to be read from the town cross at Edinburgh in 1745, proclaiming his father as James III. and himself Prince Regent. It now hangs in the hall of the College.

entrusted these jewels, together with the badges of the Garter and the orders of SS. George and Andrew, worn by the same unfortunate monarch, to Monsignor Cesarini, for transmission to England, as a personal gift to the Prince of Wales. These sad mementoes were duly forwarded by Cardinal Consalvi and suitably acknowledged by the royal recipient.

The years sped on. An empire called into existence by the sword vanished amidst the thunder of Waterloo, and with the return of peace the Prince who directed England's destinies had leisure to remember the illustrious dead. A renowned sculptor was commissioned to prepare a suitable monument to mark the resting-place of the last of the Stuarts, and in 1819 the great masterpiece of Canova, with its guardian genii, was completed. Since that time what countless strangers from these realms have mused before that sculpture on the lives its stone commemorates, and read its simple epitaph:

'JACOBO III.,
Jacobi II., Magnæ Brit. Regis Filio,
KAROLO EDVARDO,
Et HENRICO, Decano Patrum Cardinalium,
Jacobi III. Filiis,
Regiæ Stirpis Stuardiæ Postremis,
Anno MDCCCIX.
"Beati Mortui qui in Domino moriuntur."

'To JAMES III.,
Son of James II., King of Great Britain,
And to CHARLES EDWARD,
And HENRY, Dean of the Cardinals,
The sons of James III.,
Last of the royal race of Stuart,
MDCCCIX.
"Blessed are the dead who die in the Lord." '*

---

* See remarks on the Stuart monument, p. 129 (Appendix).

APPENDIX.

CARDINAL YORK's villa passed after his death into the hands of trustees, who let it as a residence to visitors attracted by the historic interest of the house, and the romantic beauty of the situation. In May, 1832, Sir Walter Scott, when seeking to recruit his shattered health in Italy, visited the villa, and was much pleased with all he saw and learned there of the last of his country's ancient kings. Mr. Edward Cheney, a Scotch gentleman, was at the time the occupant of the property, which still contained several interesting relics of the Stuart family, notably a portrait of Charles I., busts of Cardinal York and his father, the Old Chevalier; also a painting of a fête given by Cardinal York in the Piazza dei Santi Apostoli shortly after his elevation to the purple, and a small ivory head of Charles I. which had served as the top of his Eminence's walking-stick. These and other valuable souvenirs remained at the villa till the early forties, when they were disposed of by auction. We subjoin a list of articles which formerly belonged to Cardinal York, together with the names of their present owners :

1. Gold and tortoise-shell box, with a miniature of
   Cardinal York. (Recently purchased by Her

Majesty the Queen from Mr. Frederick Litch-field, of the Sinclair Galleries, Shaftesbury Avenue.)

2. Cardinal York's mitre. (Captain Anstruther Thompson.)

3. Case for mitre, with arms. (Captain Anstruther Thompson.)

4. A scarlet biretta. (Captain Anstruther Thompson.)

5. Speech of the Lord High Steward (Lord Cowper) at the trial of the Lords Derwentwater, Widdrington, Nithsdale, Carnwarth, Kenmure and Nairne. Printed by Jacob Tonson, London, 1715, fol. (Belonged to Cardinal York. Now in the possession of Lord Braye.)

6. Snuff-box of gold and red enamel. (Lord Napier and Ettrick.)

7. Bronze medal of Cardinal York. (Captain Anstruther Thompson.)

8. Silver trowel and case used by Cardinal York at the Jubilee, on the walling up of the Porta Sacra. (Lord Braye.)

9. Medal of Pius VII., belonged to Cardinal York. (Lord Braye.)

10. Note-book of Cardinal York. (Lord Braye.)

11. Touch-pieces of James III. and Henry IX. (Captain Anstruther Thompson.)

12. Cardinal York's seal. (B. R. Townley Balfour, Esq.)

13. Status Animarum Almæ Urbis, Anni 1764. An account of the parishes of Rome. MS. bound in vellum, with Cardinal York's arms on the cover. (The Misses Boyle.)

14. Maps of the invasion of Scotland by Prince Charles Edward in 1745. Printed by Juillot, Geographer Royal to Louis XV. They afterwards passed into the possession of Cardinal York. (Lord Braye.)

15. I Principi di Scozia Alessandro e Matilde. A drama by Count Giuseppe Sebastiani, dedicated to Cardinal York, whose arms are on the cover, 1780. (Lord Braye.)

16. Engraving of the Funeral Procession of King James III. at Rome, 1766. (Lord Braye.)

17. A pair of spectacles and case of Cardinal York. (Mrs. C. Markham.)

18. Diamond buckle given by Cardinal York to Sir John Coxe-Hippisley. (Henry H. Almack, Esq.)

19. Two gold keys, used by Cardinal York at the Jubilee. (Lord Braye.)

20. Snuff-box of Cardinal York. (Lord Napier and Ettrick.)

21. Gold episcopal ring, set with an amethyst, of Cardinal York. (Rev. F. G. Lee, D.D.)

22. Amber flask of Cardinal York (B. R. Townley Balfour, Esq.)

23. Silver medal of Cardinal York, with the legend, ' Non desideriis hominum sed voluntate Dei, 1788.' (Duke of Leinster.)

24. Copper medal of Cardinal York. (Duke of Leinster.)

25. Two large pictures by Leone Ghezza, one representing the marriage of the Old Chevalier and the Princess Maria Clementina by the Bishop of Montifiasconi (Sebastian Bonaventura), on

September 1, 1719, and the other the baptism of Prince Charles Edward by the same prelate, on December 31, 1720, in the presence of the Stuart Court, several Cardinals, prelates, and the representatives of the British and native nobility. (Both these fine historic paintings belonged to Cardinal York, but are now in the possession of the Earl of Northesk.)

26. Scent-bottle, with gold stopper, belonging to Cardinal York. (B. R. Townley Balfour, Esq.)

27. Various miniature portraits of the Stuart family, from Robert II., King of Scotland (died 1390), to the Princess Louisa of Stolberg. (These were collected by Cardinal York, and are now in the possession of the Earl of Galloway.)

Some Portraits of Cardinal York.

1. The Cardinal when very young. Small life size, three-quarters length figure in three-quarters view to spectator's left; eyes to front, right hand on helmet, left on hip; powdered hair, steel breastplate, buff sleeves and gloves, blue ribbon, badge of Thistle on the breast, ermine cloak. Size, 48 in. by 38 in. Painted by T. Blanchet. (In the possession of W. J. Hay, Esq., of Duns.)

2. The Cardinal when a boy. Whole length, life size, in court dress, with greyhound by his side. (Belonging at present to the Earl of Orford.)

3. Portrait of the Cardinal. Life size, three-quarter length figure, view to left, holding an open book with both hands, and turning towards the

front as if to read aloud. Cardinal's cape (mozetta), crown and mitre on cushion in front. (Duke of Hamilton, K.T.)

4. Portrait of the Cardinal in *cappa magna*. Half-length size, three-quarters view to right, holding paper in his hand. The same as the picture now in the National Portrait Gallery, of which a copy is given at the commencement of this work. (Lord Braye.)

5. The same as preceding, except that by the side of his Eminence appears a crown resting on a marble table. (Now belonging to Blair's College, Aberdeen.)

REMARKS ON THE STUART MONUMENT.

Though generally attributed to the munificence of George IV., the monument to the Stuarts in St. Peter's, at Rome, was erected almost entirely at the expense of Pius VII., since the contribution of the Prince Regent amounted to only fifty guineas.

The remains of those whom this fine piece of sculpture commemorates do not lie immediately beneath, but under the dome, in that part of the vast Basilica called the 'Grotte Vecchie.' There, in the first aisle, on the left of the entrance, against the wall, is a plain marble slab announcing the fact that 'here is the actual resting-place of James III., Charles III., and Henry IX., Kings of England.' Just opposite is the monument to Queen Maria Clementina, consisting of a porphyry pyramid by Filippo Barigioni and Pietro Bracci, erected by the Fabric of St. Peter's at a cost of 18,000 scudi.—*Notes and Queries*, February 25, 1854.

REFERENCES.

The following are the principal sources of information from which the present work has been compiled :

1. 'Female Fortitude Exemplified,' a narrative of the elopement of the Princess Clementina, published in London in 1722.

2. 'An Account of the Funeral Ceremonies performed at Rome in honour of the Princess Clementina Sobieski.' (A contemporary publication translated from the *Roman Journal* for January 29, 1735.)

3. Professor Ewald's 'Life and Times of Prince Charles Stuart' (Chatto and Windus).

4. 'Scottish Soldiers of Fortune,' by James Grant.

5. The Letters of the poet Gray.

6. 'An Incident in the History of the Stuarts,' by Father John Morriss, S.J. (In the *Month*, August, 1887.)

7. 'History of the Rebellion of 1745-46,' by W. and R. Chambers.

8. 'Tales of a Grandfather,' by Sir Walter Scott.

9. Lord Mahon's 'History of England.'

10. Diary of Cardinal York, in the Library of Stonyhurst College, Lancashire.

11. *Notes and Queries* for the years 1849-56.

12. Historical MSS. Commission Reports, 1872 to 1884.

13. 'Memoirs of the Jacobites,' by Mrs. Thompson (London, 1846).

14. 'Italy,' a descriptive work by Joseph Forsyth (London, 1812).

15. 'Six Months in Italy,' by George Stillman Hillard (London, 1853).
16. Letters of Sir Horace Mann, British Envoy at the Ducal Court of Tuscany from 1763 to 1784.
17. Various letters of Cardinal York written between 1767 and 1800.
18. 'Records of the English Province' (vols. vii., xii.), by Brother Foley, S.J.
19. 'West Grinstead et les Caryll,' by M. Max de Trenqualéon (London: Burns and Oates; Paris: Chez Monsieur Torré, 51, Rue Sainte Anne).
20. 'Pontificate of Clement XIV.,' by Fr. Augustine Theiner (Paris: Didot Frères, 1852).
21. 'Life of St. Paul of the Cross,' by the Hon. and Rev. Father Ignatius Spencer, of the Passionist Congregation (London, 1860).
22. 'Tales of the Century,' by Charles Edward and John Sobieski Stuart—'the sham Stuarts' (London, 1846).
23. 'Life of Hercules, Cardinal Consalvi' (Paris, 1864).
24. 'The Captive of Valence' (London, 1802).
25. 'Life and Times of Valentine, Lord Cloncurry' (published 1849).
26. The descriptive catalogue of the Stuart Exhibition at the New Gallery, Regent Street, London, 1888-89.

INDEX.

A.

C.

U.

V.

Z.

THE END.

R. & T. WASHBOURNE, PRINTERS, 18, PATERNOSTER ROW, LONDON.

LORD NELSON AND CARDINAL YORK.

Sir,—With reference to the above the following may be of interest. The Battle of the Nile was fought on August 1-2, 1798, and the news of the victory arrived in Naples a few weeks later. As our Minister to the Neapolitan Court, Sir William Hamilton, husband of "Nelson's Enchantress," was on his way to announce the news to the King, he met the Cardinal Duke of York out driving and introduced himself as follows: "I beg pardon of your Eminence for stopping your carriage, but I am sure will be glad to hear the good news which I have to communicate." The Cardinal: "Pray, Sir, to whom have I the honour of speaking?" "To Sir William Hamilton." The Cardinal, much pleased, then heard the account of Nelson's triumph. He charged Captain Capel, who was about to proceed with dispatches to England, to inform his countrymen "that no man rejoices more sincerely than I do in the success and glory of the British Navy."

Nelson made his triumphal entry into Naples on September 22, when the whole Court and population came forth to welcome "the saviour of Italy." As the Cardinal did not go to Venice till about May, 1799, he was undoubtedly among the noble personages who personally congratulated the illustrious hero. When the Duke of Sussex, son of George III., was at Rome in 1793, Cardinal York, who conceived a great esteem for him, presented the Duke with a cavalry sword which had been carried by his brother, Prince Charles Edward, during the rebellion of 1745-6. The Duke afterwards wore this sword when in command of the "Loyal North Britons." It may well be that the last of the Stuarts bestowed a similar mark of favour on the Victor of the Nile, though Southey, whose well-known "Life" is rather circumstantial, makes no mention of the Cardinal and Nelson having ever met—a somewhat unfortunate omission, if the contrary were the case.

Whilst engaged in researches for the short Memoir of Cardinal York which I published some years ago, I could find no assertion or even suggestion that his Royal Highness was ever on board the British Fleet, though the Mediterranean Squadron did receive positive orders to rescue Pope Pius VI., the reigning Pontiff, from the hands of the French. When the advance of the invaders compelled the Cardinal to fly from Naples, he appears to have journeyed to Venice in a Greek merchantman.

Considering Lord Nelson's long sojourn in Naples, a stay extending to some twenty months, it is in every way likely that he must have met his titular Sovereign at the Court and in general society many times. The recent victory was regarded as a direct intervention of Providence by all classes of the population; and showers of presents on Nelson were the order of the day. Such being the case, is it not strongly probable that the *de jure* Henry IX. showed his sense of appreciation of the great event, by bestowing on the illustrious Admiral the silver-mounted dirk associated with his own unfortunate brother, and the memories of the '45? Apologising for thus trespassing on your space,

I am yours faithfully,

BERNARD W. KELLY.

St. Anthony's, North Cheam.